D1342462

THE 10:30 FROM MARSEILLE

"A strongly plotted story of murder with a clever ironical ending. For a first novel it is remarkable"   ***Daily Telegraph***

"Japrisot writes with warmth, and has a gift for rendering almost every character instantly likable"   ***New Yorker***

"Sébastien Japrisot's talents as a storyteller have something of magic about them. You have to wait until the last page to be liberated from his grasp"

JEAN-MARIE GUILLAUME, *Quotidien de Paris*

Sébastien Japrisot

THE 10:30 FROM MARSEILLE

*Translated from the French
by Francis Price*

THE HARVILL PRESS
LONDON

First published with the title *Compartiment Tueurs* by Editions Denoel, Paris, 1962

First published in Great Britain by Souvenir Press, 1964

This paperback edition first published in 1998 by
The Harvill Press
84 Thornhill Road
London N1 1RD

www.harvill-press.com

1 3 5 7 9 8 6 4 2

Copyright © Editions Denoel, 1962

English translation copyright © Souvenir Press,
Editions Denoel, Sébastien Japrisot, 1964

A CIP catalogue record for this book is available from the British Library

ISBN 1 86046 440 8

Designed and typeset in Minion at Libanus Press, Marlborough, Wiltshire

Printed and bound in Great Britain by Mackays of Chatham

Half title illustration: by Newell and Sorrell

The 10:30 from Marseille

This Is the Way It Began

The train was coming in from Marseille.

To the man whose job it was to go through the corridors and check the empty compartments, it was "the Phocéen – ten minutes to eight; after that, breakfast". Before that, there had been "the Annecy – twenty-five minutes to"; he had found two raincoats, an umbrella, and a leak in the heating system. When he saw the Phocéen pull in on the other side of the same platform, he was standing by a window, looking at the broken nut on one of the valves.

It was a Saturday at the beginning of October, very clear and very cold. Travellers returning from the south, where people were still lying on the beaches and swimming, were surprised to see their breath form little clouds of vapour when they spoke.

The man who checked the corridors and compartments was forty-three years old. His name was Pierre, his political ideas were far to the left of centre, and he was thinking about a strike that was going to be called the following week. And things being what they are at 7:53 on a cold Saturday morning in Gare de Lyon, he was hungry, and looking forward to a good cup of coffee.

Since the trains would not be moved from their present location for at least half an hour, he decided, as he left the

Annecy, to go and have his coffee before taking on the Phocéen. At 7:56 he was in an office that was being repaired, at the foot of track M. There was a steaming yellow cup with a red rim in his hand, his blue cap was pushed back on his head, and he was discussing the effectiveness of starting a strike on Tuesday with a short-sighted timekeeper and a North African labourer. Tuesday was a day when no one, absolutely no one, took the train.

He spoke slowly and deliberately, emphasizing his view that a walkout was just like advertising: the important thing is to get your point across to the largest possible number of people. The others said of course, he was right. They almost always said he was right. He was a big man, heavy-set, with a deep voice and large, calm eyes that made him appear younger than he was. He had a reputation for being the kind of man who didn't swallow his teeth when someone came up behind him and clapped him on the back. He was a solid type.

At 8:05 he was going through the corridors of the Phocéen, opening the glass-panelled doors, glancing inside the compartments, closing the doors again.

In carriage No. 4, second-class, in the third compartment from the rear, he found a yellow and black scarf that had been left on one of the berths. He unfolded it, saw that it was printed with a drawing of the Bay of Nice, and recalled his own souvenirs of Nice – the Promenade des Anglais, the casino, and a little café near Saint-Roch. He had been there twice: to a summer camp when he was twelve, and on his honeymoon, when he was twenty.

He had liked Nice.

In the next compartment, he found the corpse.

The woman was stretched diagonally across the lowest of

the three berths on the right, with her legs hanging awkwardly over the edge, so that her feet were invisible. Her eyes were open, stonily reflecting the light from the open door. Her clothing – a dark suit and a white blouse – was disordered, but no more so, he thought, than that of any traveller who had slept on a second-class berth fully dressed. Her left hand was clasped tightly around the edge of the berth. Her right hand was spread out flat on the thin mattress, so that her entire body seemed to have been petrified in the act of trying to get up. The skirt of the suit had been pulled up around the knees. A black pump with a very high heel was lying on the grey SNCF blanket, which was rolled in a ball at the foot of the berth.

The man who checked the corridors swore softly and stared at the corpse for twelve seconds. The thirteenth second, he looked at the lowered blind on the window of the compartment. The fourteenth, he glanced at his watch.

It was 8:20. He swore again, wondered vaguely which one of his superiors he should notify, and began searching in his pockets for a key to lock the compartment.

Fifty minutes later, the blind had been lifted and the sun had moved around so that its rays lay across the woman's knees. Inside the compartment, the police photographer was aiming his camera at the recumbent figure, and flash bulbs were popping systematically.

The woman was brunette, young, rather tall, rather thin, and rather pretty. A little above the opening of her blouse there were two marks of strangulation on her neck. The lower one was a series of small round bruises, side by side. The upper, which was also deeper and more pronounced, was a straight line bordered with a blackish swelling. The doctor passed an index finger over it lightly, noting, and calling to the others' attention the fact that it was not just a bruise on the skin: the black came off on his finger, as if the murderer had used something old or dirty.

The three men in overcoats who surrounded him edged forwards to get a better look, and again there was a crunching sound from the pearls on the floor of the compartment. They were everywhere: lying in little patches of sunlight on the sheet around the woman, on the other lowest berth, on the floor, and even on the windowsill, two feet above the floor. One was found later in the right-hand pocket of the woman's suit. They were fake pearls, from a costume-jewellery necklace of no value.

The doctor said that at first glance it appeared that the murderer had stood behind his victim, slipped a belt or something of the sort around her neck, and strangled her by pulling on both it and the necklace, which had broken. There were no lacerations on the back of the neck, and the cervical vertebrae were not broken. On the other hand, the Adam's apple and the lateral muscles had been badly crushed.

She had defended herself feebly. Her nails were carefully manicured, and the polish was chipped on only one – the middle finger of the right hand. The murderer, either voluntarily or as a result of the struggle, had then thrown her back on the berth. He had completed the job of strangling her by pulling at the ends of the belt on either side of the neck. Insofar as it was possible to judge, she had died within the space of two or three minutes. Death had taken place about two hours earlier, at approximately the time of arrival of the train.

One of the men in the compartment, seated on the

edge of the bottom left-hand berth, with his hands in the pockets of his overcoat and his hat knocked slightly sideways on his head, muttered a question.

The doctor looked annoyed, but as a matter of duty, he lifted the woman's head, leaning over so that he could study the back of the neck, and then said that of course it was a little early to give a definite answer, but that, in his opinion, the murderer need not have been either much bigger or much stronger than his victim. A woman could have done it as easily as a man. But women were not stranglers.

That was all he could do for the moment. He would examine the corpse at the Institute later in the morning. He picked up his case, wished the man who was seated on the other berth good luck, and left. He closed the door of the compartment behind him as he went out.

The man who had spoken took his right hand from his pocket, bringing a cigarette with it. One of his companions gave him a light, then put his own hands back in his pockets and walked over to the window.

Just beneath him, on the platform, the men from the fingerprint and identification divisions were standing about, smoking silently, waiting for the compartment to be turned over to them. A little further away a group of policemen, some curious station employees and a couple of window cleaners were talking heatedly. A canvas stretcher, rolled up in its shiny wooden poles, was leaning against the railway carriage just beside the forward door.

The man looking out of the window took a handkerchief from his pocket, blew his nose, and announced that he was coming down with flu.

The man in the hat, still seated behind him, replied that that was too bad, but his flu would have to wait for a while, because someone was going to have to take care of all this. He called the man at the window Grazzi, and said that it was Grazzi who was going to do it. He got up, took off his hat, pulled a handkerchief from inside the band, blew his nose noisily, and said that, damn it, he had the flu too. Then he put the handkerchief back in the hat, and the hat back on his head, and said irritably that as long as Grazzi was going to handle it, Grazzi might just as well get started right away. Handbag. Clothing. Suitcase. First, who this female is, or was. Second, where she came from, where she lived, who she knew, and all that. Third, the list of reservations for the compartment. Report tonight at seven o'clock. A little less goofing-off than usual wouldn't do any harm. The attorney general would put that pighead Frégard on this one. A word to the wise, etc. . . . The trick is to surround it, and then pull it all together. Do you get me? Surround it.

He took his hands from his pockets and formed a circle with his arms, staring at the man by the window, but the man didn't turn around. He just said, all-right, he would have to see what's-his-name about that slot-machine business, but he could manage.

The third man, who was gathering up the pearls from the floor, looked up and asked what should he do, boss? There was a barking sound, like laughter, and then the rasping voice said he might as well string the things he had in his hands. What else was he good for?

The man with the hat turned back to the one who was still looking out of the window, Grazzi: a very tall, thin man in a navy-blue overcoat worn threadbare at the elbows, with dull brown hair and shoulders that carried the weight of thirty-five or forty years of dutiful submission. There was a cloud of smoke on the window in front of his face. He couldn't have been able to see very much.

The man with the hat said not to forget, Grazzi, to look in the other compartments; you never know, and even if you just find bricks they give weight to the report. Pull everything in . . .

He was about to say something else, but instead he shrugged and just said, damn it, he'd caught a bad one. He looked down at the man with the pearls and said, I'll see you at the office noon, *ciao*. He went out without closing the door.

The man standing in front of the window turned around. His face was very pale, and his eyes blue and peaceful-looking. He said to the other man, who was leaning over the berth that held the stiff, dead body of the woman, that some people needed a good kick in the pants.

It was a little notebook with a spiral binding and a red cover spotted with grimy fingerprints. The man who was called Grazzi by his colleagues opened it in an office on the second floor of the station, to make notes on the first statements. It was almost eleven o'clock. Carriage No. 4 of the Phocéen had been moved to a siding, with the other carriages of the train. Three men, wearing gloves and carrying cellophane bags, were sifting its contents.

The Phocéen had left Marseille on Friday 4 October at 10:30 P.M. It had made its usual stops in Avignon, Valence, Lyon and Dijon.

The six berths in the compartment where the body had been found were numbered from 221 to 226, starting from the bottom, with the odd numbers to the left as you entered and the even numbers to the right. Five had been

9

taken before the train left Marseille. Only one, 223, was empty, as far as Avignon.

The body had been lying on berth 222. The reservation stub found in the handbag indicated that she had boarded the train at Marseille, and that, unless she had changed places with someone, she had occupied berth 224 during the trip.

Tickets in the second-class carriages had been verified only once: after the stop at Avignon, between eleven-thirty and twelve-thirty. The two employees who made this check had been reached by telephone. They stated that no one had missed the train, but to their great regret, they remembered nothing at all about the occupants of the compartment.

Quai des Orfèvres, 11:35 A.M.

The clothing, underclothes, handbag, suitcase, shoes and wedding ring were laid out on a table in the inspectors' room – the wrong table, as a matter of fact. A typed carbon copy of the inventory made up by Bezard, a temporary clerk in the identification division, was with them.

A tramp who was being questioned at a nearby table made a dirty joke about a paper bag, which had been torn in the course of its travels from one office to another and now revealed a cloud of white nylon. The man called Grazzi told him to shut up, and the tramp replied that unless they were going to listen to him, he wanted to leave. At this, the inspector seated across the table from him lifted a hamlike fist, and a woman who had witnessed a traffic accident "from the beginning to the end" felt obliged to come to the help of the oppressed man. The resulting dispute was punctuated by the clatter of objects dropped by Grazzi in an attempt to move everything to his own table in one trip.

Before the incident was finally settled, Grazzi knew most of what there was to be learned from his ungainly bundles. As he worked over the inventory, portions of them spread from his table to his chair and then to the floor, and onto other tables, and the other inspectors on duty began cursing under their breath about this idiot who couldn't be satisfied with the space provided for him.

The typed inventory from the identification division was accompanied by several explanatory notes: a pearl found in the right-hand pocket of the dark suit had been sent to be examined with the others collected in the train; the finger-prints taken from the handbag, the suitcase, the shoes, and the objects inside the handbag and the suitcase were almost all those of the victim herself, and it would require some time to compare what others there were with those taken in the compartment, since they were neither clear nor recent; a button missing from the blouse had been found in the compartment and would be examined along with the pearls; a carefully folded piece of paper found in the handbag, bearing some clumsy, obscene drawings with the caption "A bird in the hand is worth two in the bush", was undoubtedly some sort of travelling salesman's vulgar riddle. And, as a matter of fact, the riddle was incorrect: from the care Bezard had taken (fourteen typed lines) to explain why it would not work out, it was easy to see that the boys upstairs had had a good time. The riddle would be the house problem for today.

By noon the riddle had, in fact, made its way through several floors of the building. The boss, sitting at his desk with his hat pushed back on his head, trying to forget his cold, had a copy of it in front of him and was proposing solutions to three laughing subordinates who had their own ideas about it.

There was a sudden silence in the room when the one they called Grazzi came in, his shoulders bowed, blowing his nose.

The boss pushed his hat back even further and said, alright, boys, he had to talk to Sherlock Holmes and from the look on his face he wasn't getting anywhere – you can run along. There was still a trace of laughter in the corners of his mouth and eyes. He picked up a pencil, placed the point on a sheet of paper covered with the drawings from the riddle, and began to fill them in carefully, while Grazzi, leaning against a radiator, deciphered the notes in his little red book in a mournful voice.

The victim's name was Georgette Thomas. Thirty years old. Born at Fleurac, in the Dordogne. Married when she was twenty, to Jacques Lange. Divorced four years later. Height 5 feet, 4 inches, brown hair, blue eyes, fair complexion, no distinguishing marks or scars. Demonstrator-saleswoman for a cosmetics firm, Barlin. Lived at No. 14, rue Duperré. Went to Marseille on a demonstrating job for the company from Tuesday 1 October to Friday night, 4 October. Stayed at the Hôtel des Messageries, rue Félix Pyat. Ate her meals in different restaurants on the rue Félix Pyat or in the business district. Earned 922 new francs a month, less social security. Bank account at the moment: 774 new francs and 50 centimes. Cash in her handbag, 324 new francs, 93 centimes, and one Canadian dollar. Robbery did not seem to be the motive for the murder. An address book still had to be checked out. Nothing particularly strange in her personal effects: an empty aspirin tube she might have meant to throw away; several photographs, all of the same child; a letter addressed "My pigeon", about a postponed rendezvous and vaguely affectionate, but undated and unsigned. That was all.

The boss said good, it was as simple as good morning, they had to get people to start shooting off their mouths. He extracted a crumpled cigarette from a pocket, straightened it out between his fingers, and began searching for a match. Grazzi struck one and held it out to him. Leaning towards the flame, the boss said first, rue Duperré, if that's really where she lived. He puffed on the cigarette, coughed, and said he ought to stop smoking. Second, the people in this Barlin outfit. Third, find her relatives and send someone to identify her.

He studied the drawings on the paper in front of him and said, with a faraway smile, that it was very funny. What did Grazzi think about this thing?

Grazzi hadn't thought about it.

The boss said okay and got up. He had to meet his son for lunch in a bistro in Les Halles. His son wanted to go to the Beaux-Arts and study God knows what. Twenty years old and nothing in his head. The trumpet and the Beaux-Arts – those were the only things he was interested in. His son was a jackass.

As he was putting on his coat, he paused, stuck out an index finger, and said Grazzi could believe him, his son was a jackass. Unfortunately, that didn't change your feelings. Grazzi could really believe him, this son of his was breaking his heart.

Grazzi said they would see each other later in the

afternoon. And what about the list of reservations, the names? The railways were never in a hurry. But there was no need to swamp the lab with a raft of examinations. Strangling some woman, that wasn't the work of a pro. Before Grazzi could say "ouf", some numbskull would fall in his lap, all cooked and ready to serve: I loved her, and all that. The trick is to pull it all together for that pighead, Frégard.

He buttoned his overcoat over a wool scarf with red checks and a stomach that made him look like a pregnant woman. He studied the knot on Grazzi's tie carefully. He never looked anyone straight in the face. Some people said there was something wrong with his eyes, something that had happened when he was a child. But who was going to believe he had been a child?

In the corridor he turned back to Grazzi, who was just going into the inspectors' room, and said he had forgotten something. This business of the slot machines: you couldn't get your fingers on it, there were too many people involved. So there was no point in building the house before they passed the logs to the boys upstairs; let them worry about it. If there were any newshounds sniffing around, butter them up with this dame – they'd like her – and shut up about the rest. A word to the wise, etc. . . .

The first newshound who came sniffing around caught Grazzi by the sleeve at four o'clock that afternoon, when he came back from a visit to rue Duperré with the blond boy who had gathered up the pearls. He had the serious smile and the prosperous look of the ones who work for *France-Soir*.

Grazzi made him a gift of the female corpse in the Gare de Lyon and then produced a bonus from his wallet: a proof of an identification photo. Georgette Thomas looked almost as she had when her body was found, carefully made-up and with her hair in perfect order, easily recognizable.

The reporter whistled, took some notes, consulted his watch, and said that he would run over to the Medico-legal Institute right away: he was "supporting" a guy there, and with any luck he could catch the concierge from rue Duperré, who had gone to identify the victim. He still had fifty minutes to get the story in for the last editions.

He left so fast that all of the other newshounds picked up the scent, and within the next half hour every news-paper in Paris knew about the story. But by then it had no interest for them; it was too late for the last editions, and the next day was Sunday.

At 4:15, unbuttoning his overcoat and preparing to get on the telephone and see where the victim's address book would lead, Grazzi saw on his table a handwritten list of the reservations for berths 221 to 226 on the Phocéen. The six travellers had reserved their places anywhere from twenty-four to forty-eight hours in advance.

221	Rivolani	Friday 4 October	Marseille
222	Darrès	Thursday 3 October	Marseille
223	Bombat	Thursday 3 October	Avignon
224	Thomas	Friday 4 October	Marseille
225	Garaudy	Thursday 3 October	Marseille
226	Cabourg	Wednesday 2 October	Marseille

One good turn deserves another. Grazzi telephoned the Medico-legal Institute to ask the reporter to include the list in his story. At the other end of the line someone asked him to hold on a minute, and Grazzi said he would.

Berth 226

René Cabourg had been wearing the same old-fashioned, belted overcoat for eight years. A good part of the year he also wore knitted wool gloves, a long-sleeved sweater, and a heavy scarf that bulged awkwardly around his neck. He was subject to recurring attacks of the flu, and as soon as the weather turned cold, his naturally sullen disposition became even more nervous and irritable.

He left the Paris-South district branch of the Progine Company ("Progress-in-your-kitchen-through-engineering") every night a few minutes after five-thirty. There was a bus stop on the Place d'Alésia just in front of the office, but he always walked to the terminus for the No. 38 at Porte d'Orléans, to be sure of getting a seat. All the way from Porte d'Orléans to Gare de l'Est he never lifted his eyes from his newspaper. He always read *Le Monde*.

This particular night – which was not a night like all the others in any event, because he had returned just that morning from the only trip he had taken in ten years – several unusual things occurred. In the first place, he left his gloves in a drawer of his desk, and since he was anxious to get home as quickly as possible – his room had not been cleaned since before he went away – he decided not to go back and get them. After that, he stopped in a brasserie at Porte d'Orléans and drank a glass of beer, which was something he never did on ordinary days. He had been thirsty ever since leaving Marseille; the compartment on the train had been overheated, and he had slept with his clothes on, because there were women and he had not been sure his pyjamas were clean. The next thing that happened tonight was that he went to three newsstands after coming out of the brasserie without finding a copy of *Le Monde*. The last edition hadn't come in yet. He gave up in the end, and bought a copy of *France-Soir*.

Seated in the No. 38 at last, in the middle, away from the wheels and next to a window, he turned the first page without looking at it. The inside pages were more sedate, and didn't irritate him quite so much. He had never liked shouting or loud laughter or vulgar stories, and large, black headlines had the same effect on him.

He was tired, and conscious of the pressure between his eyes which always preceded an attack of the flu. He had slept badly on the train; he had been afraid of falling out of the upper berth, and kept his nose buried in the sweater he had folded into a pillow because he didn't trust those provided by the SNCF. The heat had been unbearable, and even when he had dozed off he could hear the clacking of the wheels and the intermittent burst of sound from the loudspeakers in the stations. And in addition to that, he had worried about all sorts of stupid things: an accident, an exploding steam pipe, the theft of the wallet beneath his head; God knows, all sorts of stupid things.

He had left Gare de Lyon without his scarf and with his overcoat hanging open. During the whole week he was in Marseille, it had been almost like summer. He could still see the dazzling sunlight on the Canebière one afternoon at about three o'clock, when he had walked the whole length of it down to the Old Port. There had been all the bright colours of the girls' dresses, and the rustling sounds of their skirts as they walked, and that always upset him a little. Now he had the flu, all-right; there was no doubt about that.

He didn't know why it should be that way, but it always was. Probably because of the girls, because of his timidity, and his thirty-eight solitary years. Because of the envying glances he was ashamed of but could not always repress when he passed a young couple, laughing and happy. Because of the idiotic pain it caused him just to see them.

He thought of Marseille, which had been a torture worse than any springtime in Paris, and of a night in Marseille just forty-eight hours ago. The thought made him lift his eyes and look around him, like a fool. Even as a child, he had had that same reaction, wanting to be sure that no one suspected what he was thinking. Thirty-eight years old.

Two seats ahead of him in the bus, a young girl was reading *Le Monde*. He looked out the window, saw that they were already at Châtelet, and he had not really read a single line of his paper.

He would go to bed early. He would have dinner, as he always did, at Chez Charles, the restaurant on the ground floor of the building he lived in. He would put off the cleaning until tomorrow; he had all of Sunday morning for that.

He was still not reading the paper, but just staring at it mechanically, his eyes wandering from one paragraph to the next, and when he saw his own name he scarcely noticed it. It was not until two lines further on, when he saw a phrase that said something about night, berths, and a train, that he stopped.

He read the phrase then, but it told him only that

something had happened the night before, in a compartment on the Phocéen. When he went back to the line where he had seen his name, he learned that someone named Cabourg had occupied a berth in this compartment.

He had to open the paper wide and go back to the first page to find the beginning of the article. The man sitting next to him muttered something or other, irritably.

It was the photograph above the headline that really startled him. In spite of the fuzzy quality of the newspaper picture, it had the slightly shocking reality of a face you think you have seen for the last time, thank God, and then find again on the next street corner.

Beyond the grey and black of the ink, he could see the colour of her eyes, the thickness of her hair, and the warmth of the smile that had brought on everything at the very beginning of the trip last night – the unreasoning hope he had felt for a while, and the shame and disgrace of a quarter past twelve. A whiff of a perfume he had vaguely disliked came back to him, recalling the moment when the woman raised her voice, although she had been standing right next to him. When she turned around, the movement of her shoulders had been sharp and swift, like that of a boxer who has seen an opening, and her eyes were like that, too: one of the sharp-eyed little boxers in the preliminaries at the Central on Saturday nights.

There seemed to be a hard knot forming in his throat, beating to the rhythm of his pulse. He could feel it so clearly that he raised his left hand and touched his thumb and index finger to his neck. As he turned towards the window, instinctively looking for his own reflection, he realized that they were going down Boulevard de Strasbourg; they were almost at Gare de l'Est.

He read the caption beneath the photograph and a few lines of the beginning of the article, and then folded the paper. There were still a dozen or so people in the bus. He got off last, clutching the rumpled newspaper in his right hand.

As he walked across the busy square in front of the station, he recognized the sounds and smells that were a part of it and should be familiar to him, since he passed here every night, but which he had never really noticed before. A train whistled somewhere in the depths of the brightly lit building, and there was a noise of engines starting up.

They had found the woman strangled on one of the berths, after the train arrived in the station. Her name was Georgette Thomas. For him, last night, she had been only a gilt "G" on a handbag, someone who spoke in a deep, almost husky voice and had offered him a cigarette – a Winston – when they exchanged a few words in the corridor. He didn't smoke.

On the pavement on the other side of the square he couldn't stand it any longer, and stopped and unfolded the newspaper again. He was nowhere near a street light, and he couldn't see to read. Still holding the paper open in his hand, he pushed through the glass doors of a brasserie. The place was so hot and noisy that for an instant he considered turning back, but then he almost closed his eyes and went in. He found an empty place on a bench at the back, next to a couple who were talking in carefully guarded tones.

He sat down without taking off his overcoat, pushed away two empty glasses and pasteboard coasters, and spread the paper across the shiny red surface of the table.

The man and woman were watching him. They must have been about forty years old, the man perhaps a little more, and they had the worn, slightly sad expressions of two people who meet for an hour or so after work every day, even though their lives are centred somewhere else. René Cabourg thought they were ugly, even a little repulsive, because they were no longer young, because the woman's chin and neck were beginning to sag, because a husband or a band of children was probably waiting for her at home, because of everything.

The waiter came and cleared off the table. René Cabourg had to lift the newspaper out of the way of the damp cloth and watch for the moisture to disappear before he put it back. He ordered a beer, as he had at Porte d'Orléans, and as he had that morning in the bistro on the corner when he went home to leave his suitcase.

He was still thirsty, but he didn't see the glass when it was brought to him. He must have known it was there, though, because he reached out and picked it up, without taking his eyes from the newspaper. When he drank from it, two drops of beer splashed across the article.

She was a representative for a cosmetics company. She had told him that. And also that she had been in Marseille for four days. He remembered the necklace, because he had seen the clasp at the back, very close, when he leaned over her.

They had found her lying on her back, with her eyes open and her clothing disordered. He had that picture in his mind the whole time he was reading. There was a wealth of details: the skirt pulled up over her knees, the high-heeled black shoes, the marks of the broken necklace on her throat.

21

She lived in a little two-room apartment near Place Pigalle. They had already questioned the concierge.

The article said that the concierge "kept dabbing at her eyes with her handkerchief". She had been very fond of her tenant: always smiling, she was, and yet Georgette Thomas had not had a very happy life. A divorcée when she was only twenty-five. A person who worked hard, and honestly. And God knows, around Place Pigalle you could see enough of them who didn't. Of course she had men visitors, but the concierge said that was her own affair; after all, she was free, the poor little thing.

René Cabourg imagined a lamp with a red silk shade, in a room with the curtains drawn. Just the one corner of light in a big area of darkness. And whispers of sound. The man, who would be tall and good-looking, with the conceited smile of someone who is accustomed to having things come easily. And her. Between the light and the shadow, that rustling of silk, and the gleam of naked flesh, the curve of a leg or a shoulder. Her very own affair.

When he finished his beer, some more drops fell on the paper. The black shoes. The woman with the warm smile who had offered him a cigarette in the corridor. And then the sharp-eyed look and the quick movement of the shoulders, like one of the boxers at the Central. All the men who had held her in their arms, and put their hands on her hips and shoulders. And himself; the stupidity of that night in Marseille, the unbearable desire he had felt for her when he helped her take down her suitcase, and this day, ever since he had left Gare de Lyon. And now this newspaper.

He told himself he was glad she was dead, that they had found her dead.

The investigation had scarcely begun at the time the paper came out. They had a list of the other passengers in the compartment. The police hoped that they would come to the Préfecture, or go to the Commissariat nearest their homes. It was possible that they could furnish details about what had happened before the murder. That, apparently, had taken place after the train arrived in the station, in the confusion at the end of a journey. Since robbery did not appear to be the motive for the crime, Commissioner Tarquin and his associates at the Préfecture hoped to find the murderer very shortly. That was all.

René Cabourg knew that there hadn't been any confusion at the end of the journey. The passengers had stood in the corridor, trying to keep their baggage out of the way, and then they had filed out of the carriage, one after the other, perfectly peacefully. Some of the baggage was handed out through the windows. On the platform, the closer you got to the exits, the denser the crowd became, until it was all around you. People were standing on their toes and craning their necks trying to locate the friends or relatives who had come to meet them.

No one had come to meet René Cabourg. He knew that, and he had been in a hurry to leave the compartment, the train, the station. He had been the first one out of the compartment, among the first out of the carriage, and in the front rank of those for whom no one was waiting at the station.

He read the list of passengers for the fourth time, trying to fit the names and the numbers to the faces. Rivolani – that must be the man in the leather jacket, almost bald, with a little cardboard suitcase, battered and dirty at the corners. Darrès – that was the girl who had got on at

Avignon, and smiled at him in the corridor while he was talking to the woman with the "G" on her handbag. No, that couldn't be she. If Georgette Thomas was berth 224, they were numbered with odd ones on the left, and even on the right. He wasn't sure. He verified the number of his own berth.

That was it. Bottom left was the man in the leather jacket, Rivolani. Bottom right, 222, was Darrès, a blonde woman about forty, too much make-up, a leopardskin coat, or something that looked like leopard. The middle berth on the left was the girl who got on at Avignon. She was blonde too, about twenty, maybe not even that, with a light-blue coat over a little summery dress with a ribbon bow on the front. The middle berth on the right was Georgette Thomas, and René Cabourg could see her knees again, when her skirt lifted for a moment as she tried to reach her suitcase. Top left, opposite him, Garaudy. He couldn't remember anything; he hadn't noticed. Or rather, yes he had, the berth was still empty when he had stretched out on his own, about twelve-thirty. Later on, he had heard a voice over there.

He raised his eyes and saw that the waiter was standing in front of his table. He was going off duty, and wanted to collect. René Cabourg took some change from his pocket and found a token for a telephone mixed in with it. He remembered a rainy night, about two weeks before, and a booth that smelled of wet sawdust, in a bistro on Boulevard de Strasbourg, not far from here. He had tried to call a friend at the office who had told him he liked boxing. There was no answer, and he still had the token.

The waiter picked up the money, said something about Saturday nights and winter is coming, shook his head, and walked away with his napkin over his forearm, moving like a man who has been standing and walking all day.

René Cabourg looked at the photo of the woman on the first page, then folded the newspaper carefully and placed it beside him on the bench. His glass was empty. He put the token on the cardboard coaster and looked at the electric clock behind the bar. It was almost seven o'clock. The couple at the next table had left. He leaned back and rested his head against the back of the bench, closing his eyes to the glare from the neon lights.

In a way, it was that little movement that decided him. He was tired, and he could see himself on Sunday, dragging himself around with the flu, between an unmade bed and a gas ring with a leaky pipe he should have fixed a hundred years ago, and a glass that would be grimy and sticky after he had had a few slugs because he wouldn't wash it. He did not want to go home right now; that was it, that must be it. He wanted to talk to someone, someone who would listen to him, who would think him important enough to listen to, for a few minutes at least.

He grasped the token in his right hand, stood up, and looked around the room, which was becoming noisy again, trying to find the telephone booth. It was downstairs.

He walked down the steps. The booth was a large one, with several phones, and the partitions were covered with scrawled notes and obscene drawings. He realized suddenly that he didn't know whom to call. The paper had said the Préfecture, or the Commissariat nearest your home.

He found a directory, with the cover torn off, and looked up the number of the Préfecture. He thought about the dead woman's knees, and what the paper had said about the way she looked: the black shoes, the marks of the necklace on her throat. He tried not to think about what he was doing. Would he be the first of the passengers in the compartment to call?

His voice went hoarse when he said "Hello", and he had to clear it by coughing. He said that he was a passenger on the Phocéen, a passenger in the compartment there was a story about in *France-Soir*, that he was Cabourg. In spite of himself, he pronounced the last words in a tone so stilted and pretentious that the voice on the other end of the line said, "So what?"

They didn't know anything about it. They told him to hold on and they would find out; but in the first place, it wasn't this number he should have called. He said he didn't know; it was the number in the book.

He waited, leaning on the shelf beneath the telephone, his chin resting in the palm of his hand, the receiver buzzing in his ear, wishing he hadn't called.

He tried desperately to think about the trip, to remember everything and decide on what he was going to say. But the only thing he could recall was the way the little girl who got on at Avignon had smiled at him. What was her name? He didn't even remember that.

He had boarded the train half an hour before departure time. Who had been in the compartment then? No one. Yes – a boy, a boy of about sixteen. Blond, unhappy-looking, wearing a rumpled tweed suit. Not exactly in the compartment – by the door. Someone from the next compartment.

René Cabourg had taken off his overcoat the first thing and stretched it out on his berth, the upper one on the right. The man in the leather jacket and the blonde woman had arrived just as he climbed down; he had been afraid they might say something, because he had rested a foot on the lower berth without taking off his shoes.

Georgette Thomas had arrived much later, just a minute or two before the train pulled out. He had been in the corridor. He had had a hard time making room for her to get into the compartment, because the corridor was crowded with passengers leaning out of the windows, saying goodbye. He had noticed her perfume, and had thought that it was too bad there were women – he wouldn't be able to undress. And then he had thought something else, something stupid; he had told himself at the time that it was stupid, and now he had forgotten it.

"I haven't forgotten about you," the voice at the other end of the line said. "I'll give you the right extension in a minute. Don't hang up."

Perhaps the others hadn't read the newspaper yet, and no one else had called? For some reason he had a feeling of familiarity, of going back to something he knew: the compartment, the berths, the trip together, with each person making out as best he could. They might bring them all together again as witnesses, to compare their stories. They would be sitting side by side on a bench in some drafty room, and they would all be nervous and a little anxious.

"All-right," said a voice on the phone, "go ahead now."

René Cabourg repeated that he was one of the passengers on the Phocéen, that they had listed his name in *France-Soir*.

There was a short, sharp buzzing that hurt his ears. Then still another voice: Commissioner Tarquin had not come back; they would connect him with Inspector Grazziano. René Cabourg remembered an American boxer, a middleweight, about the same time as Marcel Cerdan. The inspector had the same name as the boxer.

Just above the shelf where he was resting his elbows there was a drawing he hadn't noticed before, crude but unmistakable, and a couple of lines of writing saying that J. F., twenty-two years old, was here every afternoon at four o'clock. J. F. didn't know how to spell. René Cabourg turned his head and saw that the same sort of notices were posted all around him. Then there was another voice on the receiver.

"Inspector Grazziano?"

Yes, it was. And he did know about it. He called him Monsieur Cabourg, like the clients he talked to all day from his office on Place d'Alésia. The voice was deep and rich, a radio announcer's voice. René Cabourg had a fleeting picture of heavy shoulders, sleeves rolled up on muscular forearms, and a hard face, lined with the fatigue of work at seven o'clock at night.

The inspector with the boxer's name said that he was getting something to write with, and then that he was listening, but a minute later he was the one who was talking, asking questions: name, age, address, profession . . .

"Cabourg, René Cabourg. Thirty-eight. I'm a sales superintendent for a company that makes household appliances. Progine. 'Progress-in . . .' Yes, that's it, Progine. No, I'm in a brasserie in front of Gare de l'Est. I live in rue Cinord, right near here. As soon as I saw the article __ . Well, not exactly, nothing special, but I thought I should call you."

The inspector was glad he had. Let's see, he had occupied berth 226, was that right?

"Yes, the upper one on the right as you go in."

"And you got on the train at Marseille?"

"That's right. Last night."

"And you didn't notice anything special, anything strange, during the trip?"

It was on the tip of his tongue to answer that this was the first trip he had made in ten years and everything about a train seemed "special" to him, but in the end he just said, no, nothing.

"When did you get off the train?"

"Just after it arrived – almost immediately."

"And when you left the compartment, you didn't notice anything special?"

Now the word made him want to laugh; it was incongruous, almost indecent. He said, no, nothing, but he could assure them that at that time the woman was still alive.

"Did you know the victim?"

"Do you mean do I know which woman it was? I saw her photo . . ."

"There were other women in the compartment?"

They didn't know that. So no one else had called. It gave him an odd feeling: the first one in the compartment, the first to leave, the first witness.

"Yes, two others. At least, I saw two."

"I only have the last names on my list," Inspector Grazziano said, "and you're the first passenger to telephone. Can you give me some description of the others?"

René Cabourg said, of course, but he had left the newspaper upstairs; he didn't remember the names. He was annoyed with himself, but at the same time he felt vaguely disappointed. He hadn't realized he would have to answer all these questions over the telephone, in a stuffy booth.

"Look, wouldn't it be better if I came to see you?"

"Now?"

There was a moment's silence, and then the radio announcer's voice said that was very obliging of him, but it was after seven o'clock, and he still had work to do on another case himself. The best thing would be for an inspector to come to see him at home the next morning; or perhaps he could come to Quai des Orfèvres about ten o'clock. Would that be inconvenient?

René Cabourg said, no, of course not, and then was ashamed because he had said it so quickly, and said he would try to change another appointment.

"Fine. If you don't have the paper, I'll give you the names of the other passengers, and their places. Try to remember. Rivolani, bottom berth on the left. A man or a woman?"

"A man. He was wearing a leather jacket. Green, I think. He had a cheap suitcase, an old one. At least, it was all scuffed on the corners. He didn't talk much. He went to bed straight away, in his clothes, and he must have gone to sleep."

"How old?"

"Forty-five, fifty. He looked like someone who works with his hands, a mechanic or something like that. This morning, before we got in, he was still sleeping when I went to wash. I had to queue to get to the lavatory – you know how it can be. After I went back, I really didn't notice him again."

The inspector said that was all-right, he had what he needed. Darrès, bottom right?

A woman, forty, maybe older. It's hard to say, because of her make-up. A leopard coat, or an imitation. He had never been able to recognize furs. She was blonde, wore a lot of perfume, and had a nice voice, clear. She seemed (he hesitated over the word sophisticated; he wasn't sure a policeman would understand), she looked as if she had been around – you know. She went to the lavatory to undress about an hour after the train left Marseille. When she came back, she was wearing a pink dressing gown over pink pyjamas. She took some kind of lozenges for her throat, and she had even offered one of them to the victim.

He was talking too much. It was the same thing in the office; he never knew how to keep to the essentials. He said that was all, and at the same time he remembered that the blonde woman had talked about films, the Côte d'Azur, and acting, and also that she had been the first one up in the morning. When he got down from his berth, she was dressed and ready to leave, with her suitcases on the floor beside her. He added these details.

The inspector said good, during the evening they had learned about an actress named Eliane Darrès; perhaps she was the woman.

Bombat, middle left?

A young girl, blonde, not very tall, pretty, about twenty. She had got on at Avignon. She looked like a typist or a secretary who had found a job in Paris. Her voice was pretty, sort of musical, but it may have been just the accent.

Garaudy, top left?

He didn't know. The berth was empty.

The inspector said that was odd, all the tickets had been punched, and according to the laboratory reports he had in front of him, the berth had definitely been occupied.

René Cabourg said the inspector had misunderstood – what he meant was that he hadn't seen anyone. When he had gone to bed himself, the berth was empty.

"What time was that?"

It was senseless. Without even hesitating, he lied.

"Eleven o'clock, eleven-fifteen. I don't know. Later on, I heard a voice. I don't sleep well anyway, and I hardly slept at all on the train."

"You heard the voice of the person in the opposite berth, Garaudy, is that right?"

"Yes. At least, I imagine it was her voice. She must have been talking to the girl in the berth below. I think, as a matter of fact, that she leaned over and they talked for quite a while."

"Why do you say 'she'?"

"Because I think it was a woman."

"What makes you say that?"

"It was a soft voice, not a man's. And then – it's hard to explain, but I don't sleep well, and I could sort of feel her presence when she moved. It was a woman."

"You mean it was just the voices and movements you heard that make you think that?"

"That's right."

The inspector asked him about the victim. René Cabourg was thirsty again. The air in the booth was stifling. He could feel his shirt sticking to his back, and drops of sweat running down his forehead and his jaw.

He had talked to Georgette Thomas for a few minutes in the corridor. She had only told him that she was a representative for a cosmetics firm. Not her name. Yes, she did say that she had been in Marseille for four days. It was her third trip to that city this year. No, she had seemed perfectly calm, very relaxed.

In the morning, she was still in the compartment when he had left. They were all still there. No, that wasn't right,

Garaudy wasn't there. He had said they were all there because he had never seen her; he didn't think of her as one of the people in the compartment at all.

He gave the number of his building in rue Cinord, the telephone number of his office, and promised to be at Quai des Orfèvres tomorrow morning at ten. Room 303, third floor.

The radio announcer's voice signed off with a word of thanks, and there was a click in the receiver. It ended the conversation, but it didn't release René Cabourg.

He read another one of the inscriptions as he was opening the door, and then stood outside the booth for a minute, breathing in the cooler air.

That's what he was. One night on a train, at a quarter past twelve, that's what he had been: someone low enough to scribble obscenities on walls. He hadn't scribbled on walls, but it came to the same thing.

Grazziano. Standing in the darkness in the square up in front of Gare de l'Est, with the collar of his overcoat turned up, René Cabourg wondered if the inspector would have talked to some of the other passengers before the next morning, and would consider him a scribbler, a sex maniac.

He had been wrong to lie about the time he went to bed. What good would it do? One of the others must have heard – she had raised her voice, she had been almost shouting. They would know there had been an argument in the corridor; they might have different ideas about what it was, or what it meant, but they would remember the time. It was after the tickets were taken, not before.

A lie. And since he had lied once, they wouldn't believe him again. He had tried to hide it, so now they would think

33

the argument must have been important. They might even find a motive in that: the bitterness of a sick mind. They wouldn't have any trouble finding a reason for the argument, and that could have been a motive too. He could easily have got off the train, come back a minute later, surprised the woman in the black shoes, alone in the compartment, and attacked her. She would have tried to defend herself. And he would have strangled her, to prevent her from screaming.

No.

Standing in front of the mirror over the basin in his top-floor room, where everything – his clothing, the rubber plants, the dishes – had gathered dust for a week, René Cabourg swallowed two pills for the flu, with a glass of water, and said no, it wouldn't happen like that the next morning.

In the first place, he could easily have been mistaken about the time he went to bed, without making it a lie. The important thing was to tell them about the argument himself, before someone else did, as if it were just an unimportant detail.

He could see the gestures he ought to use, the casual attitude he should assume. He would skip over the incident very quickly, smiling and shaking his head, letting them know what he was thinking: "Women, after all . . ."

He would say, "Women, after all . . ." He would say, "There we were, just the two of us, alone in the corridor. She wasn't bad-looking, and – well, you know what I mean. A man can tell about things like that most of the time, but sometimes you're wrong. You know what I mean. Well, anyway, she got up on her high horse, so I went to bed."

He would go on to something else very quickly. It would

34

be a joke between men, nothing more. He could even say that it was too bad a broad who was built like that should get herself knocked off in a railway station.

Looking at himself in the mirror, almost the way he had looked at the drawing in the phone booth, without really seeing anything, he suddenly felt even more depressed than he had then. He knew he couldn't play that part, or use those words. He would make a fool of himself again. He would blurt out the truth of his own accord – something so miserable, so wretched, that they would all be embarrassed. He would stammer, he would blush, he might even cry. They would have to help him on with his overcoat, and then they would push him out the door because they wouldn't know what to say, and they would all breathe easier when he was gone. A poor slob.

René Cabourg, who had taken off his overcoat, put it on again and buttoned it. He wasn't going to stay here. He would go and get something to eat; it didn't matter what. He saw his suitcase on the bed, which had not been made since the Saturday before, and thought that it would be a good idea to put on a clean shirt and get out another pair of gloves. But he didn't do it. He went out, turning out the overhead light but forgetting the other one, the one above the basin, still lighting an empty mirror.

He hesitated a moment before the door of Chez Charles. It was almost nine o'clock. He could see the proprietor through the window, counting money at the desk. There was only one customer, a blond young man who lifted his head and stared at him, with mouth open to swallow a piece of steak. René Cabourg walked away, turning up the collar of his coat, thrusting his hands into his pockets.

As he walked, he thought about the woman in the

dark suit, about the long, nylon-sheathed legs, and the way *France-Soir* said she had been found. He wished he hadn't left the newspaper on the bench in the brasserie. He would have liked to read the article again, see the photo again.

Why, in God's name, had he telephoned? There must be dozens of people named Cabourg in this dreary city. It had never really been his city, anyway. Grazziano would never have found him.

Grazziano made him think of the boxer, and the boxer of the Central. The Central on Saturday nights. Tonight was Saturday.

He had the feeling that this was the first pleasant thing that had occurred to him in a very long time. The Central.

He thought at first of taking the metro, and then, what the devil, it was still early in the month, he still had some money, and he would get a raise at Christmas. He started towards Gare de l'Est, almost running, looking for a taxi.

By the time he reached the station he was running, and someone who was doubtless trying to catch a train was running behind him. René Cabourg bumped into a passing couple, apologized hastily, and shouted to the driver of a cab as he opened the door, "The Central . . . The boxing arena."

He was out of breath. Nine o'clock. The fights would have started already; he would miss the first one. It was a first one, a three-round amateur match, that had been the start of these Saturday-night evasions of reality. In 1957. A night in February. Two bantamweights, 117 pounds; little men with the faces of little animals.

He had gone to the Central with an old school friend who was spending a week in Paris and then going back to the Gironde, where they had both been born. At first he had just watched it, the wary blows, the looks on the little men's faces when they backed away to catch their breath. But it wasn't that. When one of the two, who had climbed straight into the ring with a towel over his shoulders, had fallen, his face crushed against the canvas, and then tried to get up, with his arms tangled in the ropes, and the other one had gone on punching and punching, until the referee pulled him away and lifted up his arm, and there was a great roar, and the noise of chairs falling over, and the crowd swelling up like an enormous wave. That was when it had happened. Just at that moment.

René Cabourg had risen with the others and shouted with them, watching the defeated fighter trying to rise, listening to the panting breath of the winner; and later, much later, he had noticed that his hands hurt from applauding, and he had become himself again – nothing, a face in a crowd.

He had gone back to the Central alone, and the same thing had happened again. Later on, there were the people you got to recognize and talk to, the forecasts you exchanged, the glass of beer you had in the bistro next door during the interval, the pleasure of Saturday night, and the thought that, after another solitary week, there would be another Saturday night.

As he got out of the taxi in front of the Central, René Cabourg thought that, for once, he would be the last person in. But no. Another taxi stopped behind his, and a woman got out, alone. She reminded him of the woman on the train; she had dark hair too.

He watched her as she approached the ticket booth. She was young, though she no longer looked it, with a little black wrap around her shoulders and a handbag she held clutched against her breast, as if she were afraid of losing it. He could see her hands, and they were red and chapped, from washing things probably; clothes and dishes. Perhaps she was the wife of one of the boxers, and would wait in the corridor outside the dressing rooms after the fight, with her head full of crazy dreams for her man; the big prizes, the comfortable apartment, the title, a chance for the future.

He watched three amateur bouts without finding any of the pleasure he had been looking for. He found himself thinking instead about the night in Marseille, forty-eight hours ago, in the little hotel on Avenue de la République: the shabby room, because he had to be careful of how much he spent, the bed that smelled of laundry soap, and the couple in the room next door, their argument and what had followed the argument. He had just come in. He still had his briefcase in his hand, filled with the files he was working on. He had sat down on the bed, perfectly still, scarcely daring to breathe, listening . . .

He had stayed there a long time, two hours, perhaps even three. He heard them laughing, he knew that they were lying on the bed on the other side of the paper-thin wall. He knew things about the woman that only her lover knew. That she was still wearing a pearl necklace, for instance. She had bought it in Paris. That her hair was very long, and hung down her back. They laughed, they argued again, and then there was silence again, and the woman had laughed.

He had never seen that woman. He had gone out and wandered endlessly through the empty streets, and when he came back he didn't hear them any more. They had left.

The crowd around him was getting up. It was the interval. He didn't dare look at the faces of his neighbours;

he didn't want to see anyone. He went down to the toilets and ran cold water over his forehead. It was burning. He was stupid to have come out. He had a fever. He was going to be ill.

Tomorrow morning he would go to see the inspector, room 303, third floor. He would tell him exactly what had happened. That he was alone, that he was ugly, that he had always been that way, that in Marseille he had learned from a woman he didn't know, through a wall in a hotel room, that he was a fool. Just like that, a fool. That after that he had walked for hours, that he had sat down on a bench and wept, God knows where, somewhere in the Marseille night. That he had never understood anything about life, about the part of it all the others enjoyed so much. They had learned the rules – God knows how, but they had learned them – and he never had. And then, after that, he had been in a night train where everything seemed new to him, "special"; that a dark-haired woman had shown him her knees when she climbed up for her suitcase to get a tube of aspirin she had never used. And he, poor fool, had convinced himself that the aspirin was just an excuse, a means of starting a conversation. That she was beautiful – he had never been so close to a woman so beautiful. That she was so close to him he could smell her perfume and see the clasp on her pearl necklace. That the necklace had reminded him of another one, one he had never seen. And that at one moment, when she was leaning out of the window of the train, talking and laughing about something, God knows what, because he hadn't heard her, he had shown that he didn't know the rules, that he was a fool.

René Cabourg did not hear the door of the gents open

behind him. He was bent over the chipped and dirty basin, the tap running, his forehead and hair dripping water, his overcoat opened on a jacket spotted with water, when the bullet hit him in the back of the neck, just a little above the shoulders. He didn't hear the report, or see the flame, or even notice another presence in the deserted room. The interval had been over for almost quarter of an hour.

He fell forwards at first, towards the mirror above the basin, not understanding why his own face was coming nearer, not feeling any pain, still thinking of what he would say the next morning. He pivoted slowly as he slipped towards the basin, and his tie dragged through the running water. He was thinking that he would tell them all, yes, when she leaned out of the window he had not done the things he would have done if he had known the rules; he had been drowning in a sea of futile hope, his head in the water from the tap, on his knees on the tiled floor of the gents, and he had put his hand on her shoulder, yes, *on her shoulder*, because she was the only person who might have understood; and she had turned on him like a boxer who has seen an opening, perhaps to make fun of him, but when she saw his face she must have seen something, he didn't know what, something unbearable, because she had been furious, she had shouted at him.

He slipped slowly down from the basin, his eyes closing when the water no longer ran over his face, telling himself, yes, my hand on her shoulder, like that, wondering what she could have seen in his face, but before he could find the answer he was stretched flat on the tiles, and he was dead.

Berth 224

Georgette Thomas had been smiling for the photographer, doing just as he instructed. She was wearing a suit with a collar of white fur that day, and it made the dark hair that framed her face seem even darker and more beautiful. She must have been proud of her hair; spent a lot of time in front of the mirror brushing and combing it, trying different arrangements. When she shopped, she probably selected things on a basis of how well they would show it off; that was why there was so much white in her wardrobe.

The man in the undershirt and pyjama bottoms – Antoine Pierre Emile Grazziano, called Grazzi – reflected that the boss was undoubtedly right. For such a pretty girl to be murdered, the motive must have been passion, and who knows, the murderer–lover might even now be sobbing his heart out in some neighbourhood Commissariat.

He put the identity photo back in his red morocco wallet – a Christmas present from his wife three years ago – and sat for a while at the kitchen table, resting his elbows on the table and his chin on his hands. He could reach the stove without getting up from his chair, and before putting on the coffee he had opened the flowered curtains at the window and looked out on a Sunday that could have been any day in the week, weighted down by a shabby, grey-black sky.

The night had left the first frost of the season on the meagre grass of what was called "the garden area" of the apartment buildings. Grazzi had told his son he would take him to Vincennes Zoo that afternoon, and when he saw the frost he didn't feel quite so bad about breaking the promise. He would try to come home for lunch – he might be able to keep one of the Préfecture cars – and stay with Dino until it was time for his nap. That would be almost the same.

The Italian coffeemaker was beginning to whistle at him. He reached out, turned off the gas, brought the pot back to the table in the same motion, and filled one of the two cups in front of him. The steam from the coffee rose in little threads before his face.

It was black and bitter, and as he drank he thought about the apartment on rue Duperré: small, neat, well furnished, and smelling almost sickly sweet, like all the apartments of women who lived alone. Then his thoughts went back to the report he had made the night before, and the pompous phrases of Commissioner Tarquin, his boss. First, put yourself inside this woman's skin, get to know her better than she knew herself, become her twin. Get to understand her from the inside out, if you see what I mean.

They had all seen very well. One of the other inspectors, Mallet, had seen Grazzi so clearly in Georgette Thomas' skin and clothing that he was still laughing when they said good night, at about eight-thirty, in the corridor outside the office. He had said, *ciao*, old girl, and wished him luck with his boy friends.

There wasn't much doubt that she had had several. Grazzi hadn't meant to do it, but in making his report in the boss's office, he had implied that she changed her lovers as often as she did her stockings.

She had a lot of stockings, very good ones, and well taken care of, all marked at the top with a little red "G", the kind of marking they use in girls' boarding schools. It had been on everything: the blouses, the slips, even the handkerchiefs. Two big drawers filled with white nylon and lace. When they searched through it, it was so soft and filmy to the touch that Grazzi, who was tall and thin, had had the feeling that his hands were hams. And there was that little red letter on everything.

At seven o'clock at night, in the room with the boss and the others, Grazzi had expressed himself badly. That wasn't really correct, though; the thing was that he had been trying to extract something to say from the nothing in his notebook, so he had expressed a conclusion that was not his own. While they were going through the cupboards and drawers in rue Duperré, Gabert, the youngster who was with him, had said, because he was young, that the girl had been pretty, and he was reading her letters and touching her clothes, "She seems to have had a pretty good time."

There were three men in the murdered woman's life – four, if you counted the ex-husband, and she hadn't seen him in months. The car salesman, Harrault, who had come to the Quai at about six o'clock, looking pale and worried. The apprentice something-or-other, Bob whatever-it-was, whom Grazzi was going to see this morning. And the boy on the fifth floor, a student. The concierge seemed to adore him.

Of the three, the only one he knew so far to have been her lover was Harrault, who put old American cars back together and sold them in a garage at Porte Maillot. A big man with a face like a thug, getting fat and flabby now. Surprisingly enough, after seeing that face, there was nothing on him in the files. In phrases that went two steps forwards and three steps back, he had admitted, okay, yes, they had "known each other for a little while". He had lowered his voice at this point, perhaps because he was speaking of the dead, or perhaps because he was married now and this was ancient history.

Grazzi had kept him for twenty minutes. Face like a thug. But no record. Unbreakable alibi for the first four days of October, and for the Saturday of the murder. A deal with a woman about a little Fiat (new, not used, and Grazzi couldn't remember how he happened to know that). Papers in order. Well dressed. Shoes shined. Ex-sales manager for a perfume company. That's where he had met Georgette Thomas, Georgette Lange at that time, a sales representative for the same company. Six months together before her divorce, two and a half years after: "known each other for a little while". Didn't know anything. Didn't know of any enemies. Didn't know of any friends. Didn't understand how it could have happened. Didn't understand anything about anything. Terribly sorry for her. Face like a thug.

Grazzi poured coffee into the other cup on the table, added two lumps of sugar and got up, rubbing the back of his neck thoughtfully. He had heard his wife stirring in bed.

The cup was too full, and while he was navigating the narrow passage between the kitchen and their bedroom, some of the coffee spilled into the saucer. He held back the word that came to his lips; he didn't want to wake the boy.

Her eyes were open; they always were. Grazzi, who slept like a log and knew that she got up at night to be sure that Dino was all-right, or to bring him a drink of water, had the feeling that she never slept.

"What time is it?" she asked him.

"Seven o'clock."

"You're going to work today?"

He said he had to, but he didn't feel right about saying it. The fact was, he didn't really have to go. He could have told Cabourg, Bob whatever-it-was, and Georgette Thomas' family to come in on Monday. No one was on his back; no one would have said anything. If the murderer used the day to run, to put some distance between him and the police, so much the better – he might just as well have confessed right away. They would look for him, and they would find him.

No, there was no reason why he had to go, except his own lack of assurance, the need he had to keep ahead of his work, like a backward scholar cramming for an exam right up to the last minute.

His wife, Cécile, knew him very well, so she simply lifted her shoulders, said nothing about the trip to the zoo, and took out her annoyance on the coffee. It was too weak, or too sweet; she wasn't sure which, but it was.

"What did they give you this time?" she said.

"A woman who was strangled in a train, at Gare de Lyon."

She handed him the cup, knowing without asking that he didn't want a case of this kind on his hands, that now he was going to be more nervous than ever, because he would be on his own; there wouldn't be anyone above him.

"Tarquin isn't going to handle it?" she said.

"He has that slot-machine business. And besides, he doesn't want to take on something he isn't sure of; not now. If everything goes all-right, he'll take the credit. If it doesn't, it's my fault. He's due for a promotion in January; he's not going to get his feet wet now."

Shaving in front of the mirror, Grazzi thought about Georgette Thomas' apartment again. It was very different from his own, but there was nothing strange about that. Hers was the apartment of a single woman, in an old building near Place Pigalle, and his was a "two rooms, kitchen and bath" in a brand-new housing development in Bagneux, with a three-year-old boy using it for a playground.

It was the atmosphere of that apartment, the pastel-tinted obscurity, the way the daylight seemed to have been shut out deliberately, that had made him say things the night before that he didn't really think – things that he at least had no reason to think. The flowered curtains at the windows, the flounces on the bed cover, the little tables and the fragile ornaments everywhere – it was typical of any young secretary, getting older and turning into an old maid. A tiny little kitchen, with everything in its proper place. A fantastic bathroom that must have cost her a small fortune to install, tiled in pink and white and smelling of creams and powders and expensive soap. A short night-dress, just like the one in her suitcase, hanging on the back of the door. Towels as thick and soft as fur, in pale colours, and all initialled "G". A white rubber cap hanging on the tap of the shower, and an assortment of little jars on a dressing table. But especially the mirrors. There were mirrors everywhere, even in the kitchen. The bedroom was so small, the bed itself took up so much space, that the number of mirrors and the way they were hung seemed very odd.

Grazzi drew his razor across the line of his jaw, leaving a broad path of clear skin visible through the lather. There had been a razor at her apartment, too, in the medicine chest, but that didn't mean anything; all women had one.

There had also been a lot of letters, most of them from the car salesman, and some photographs of men, in an old biscuit tin, along with some of herself and her family.

But that wasn't it. There was something else in that apartment. He didn't know quite what, he couldn't put his finger on it, but it was there; it had impressed itself on him, and it had been that that made Gabert say, "She seems to have had a pretty good time." The cloying intimacy of the bedroom, its exaggerated femininity perhaps. Or the splendid bathroom. Or that absurd little red letter marking everything, like a schoolgirl's wardrobe.

His wife came into the bathroom and took her dressing gown from its hook on the door. Grazzi watched her in the mirror and gestured vaguely with the razor.

"Cécile . . ." he began, and hesitated. "What do you make of a woman who marks everything, all of her clothing, with her initial?"

"Maybe she sends it out to be washed."

"It's the initial of her first name. And besides, you don't send out things like stockings and slips to be washed, do you?"

Cécile didn't think so. She stood beside him and looked at herself in the mirror, running her fingers through her hair.

"I don't know. I know there are women who have all of their things embroidered. I've seen that."

47

He explained that this wasn't embroidery, it was just a little square of cloth with an initial, the kind of thing you sewed in the lining. When he was a boy at school in Le Mans, his mother had marked his pyjamas and handkerchiefs and everything else the same way. With him it hadn't been an initial, though; it had been a number. He remembered it: eighteen.

Cécile didn't know. She said there must be a reason. The woman might be a little crazy. In any case, she had other things to think about. The boy was going to wake up at any minute, and he wasn't eating well. It wasn't good for a three-year-old child never to see his father at meals. Would Grazzi be home for lunch?

He promised that he would be, thinking about the child's not eating well, and also about Georgette Thomas, sitting in a chair beside one of the little tables, sewing a little red "G" on lace-trimmed white nylon.

He took the bus that came in from l'Hay-les-Roses, empty on a Sunday morning, and stood on the open platform at the back, so he could smoke his first cigarette. At Porte d'Orléans, where he had to change, there was none of the usual commotion of nine o'clock. The sky was beginning to turn blue, and the streets of Paris had more of a holiday air than those in Bagneux.

In the No. 38 bus, he sat down. As they passed Place d'Alésia, he noticed the sign on the front of the Progine office and remembered that at ten o'clock he was supposed to see the man who had called last night – what was his name? Cabourg. And Gabert might have found the others. The actress, Darrès. And Rivolani. There were only two Rivolanis in the telephone book.

Grazzi thought of the youngster, Gabert, sitting at the telephone in the office until after midnight, dialling numbers one after the other, apologizing, explaining, trying to straighten out misunderstandings. And when Grazzi arrived in a little while, all he would have to say would be, "Nothing, chief. Seventy-three calls, twelve invitations to go to hell, two madmen, and a grocer who had to be at the market at four o'clock in the morning and didn't think much of cops who call at eleven o'clock at night."

"I found three of the others, chief," Gabert said.

He was sitting on the corner of a table that rightfully belonged to Pardi, a taciturn Corsican who always worked alone and had wound up a nasty abortion case just the day before. Gabert's freshly shaved cheeks were still pink from the cold outside; he looked as though he had just woken up.

Grazzi took off his overcoat as he walked over to his own table, and nodded to the two duty inspectors who were standing in a corner, smoking and talking about a football game. A man in a threadbare jacket with no tie was sitting by the door with handcuffs on his wrists, looking bewildered.

Without lifting his eyes from the game he carried with him everywhere (a puzzle in mathematics, numbers to be moved around on a little metal square until you found the solution and started all over again on another set), Gabert said that he hadn't gone to bed until after midnight, and the state had lost thousands of francs in telephone calls again, and the stupidity of people was unbelievable.

"Which ones did you find?" Grazzi asked.

"The actress, first. An answering service. She was out to

49

dinner; they didn't know where. Thirty restaurants, before I found her at Chez André. Christ, it makes you hungry, telephoning restaurants. All the noises you hear."

"Who else?"

"Rivolani. He's the one we thought, the truck driver. I spoke to his wife, not him. He was making a delivery to Marseille, and the truck broke down about twenty kilometres before he got there. He left it in a garage in Berre and took the train back. His wife has a nice voice."

"And the third?"

"The third *is* a woman, and the berth *was* occupied."

"Garaudy?"

Gabert had found the solution to one game, scrambled the numbers, and started another. His index finger moved so fast it made Grazzi dizzy to watch him. His blond hair, meticulously combed and waved, was still damp at the temples. He hadn't been up long. He was still wearing the beige overcoat with the hood at the shoulders, his "duffel coat" he called it, and the tartan scarf that "actually came from Scotland". A dozen times a day the other inspectors pulled his leg about that coat and his hair and his rich boy's manners, but it didn't seem to bother him at all. He was fairly short, and thin, with a smile that said he didn't take anything very seriously, and certainly not his profession. He didn't particularly like it, but he didn't dislike it either. It just wasn't important to him.

"Madame Garaudy, yes," he said. "One of several Madame Garaudys. This one's husband is one of the sons, an engineer who was transferred to Marseille six months ago. Twenty-six years old, a specialist in electronics, supposed to be a hotshot. Electronics is a funny thing. I've got a friend who's involved in it. According to him, you can solve all of Greek mythology with those machines."

Grazzi was sitting at his table, with the little red notebook in front of him. He scratched the back of his neck impatiently.

"So?" he said.

"So, they've been married for a year. A big long story about all the trouble the mother-in-law went to to get them settled in Marseille."

"All-right, let's get on with it."

"It's important — that's why she was on the train, alone. They left all sorts of things in Paris, when they moved down there. The husband is a supervisor — stays at the plant days at a time, sleeps with the machines — so Madame came up alone to see about shipping all the kitchen stuff, and to kiss her mother-in-law."

"So?"

"Chief, you're being hard to get along with. It took me two hours to learn all that. I finally managed to talk to the daughter-in-law, the one you're interested in. She was having dinner in Neuilly with some more of the Garaudy clan. Shook all over when I told her what had happened; I could hear it. What a story to tell the family: "I wasn't the one who was strangled, but I might have been . . ." Her name is Evelyne. She has a nice voice, too. I asked her to tell me what she looks like, just to amuse myself. She must be all-right. She'll be here for a few days — until Thursday, I think. I told her we would have to ask her some questions."

Gabert laughed, without looking up from the game or interrupting the flying movements of his finger.

"She swore that she didn't do it; she hadn't strangled anyone. I told her we'd see about that. If the chief agrees,

51

I'm going to talk to her at eleven o'clock – 130, rue La Fontaine, ask for Lyne. Do you agree?"

Grazzi said that was better than having her hanging around here all morning, but not to take the car, he needed it to go home for lunch.

At ten o'clock Cabourg had not arrived, so Grazzi decided to go and have a cup of coffee in the café at Pont Saint-Michel. Just as he was leaving the room with Gabert, a policeman came to tell him that there were a man and a woman who wanted to see him, the sister and brother-in-law of the murdered woman. Their name was Conte. They had just come from the Medico-legal Institute.

The Contes sat down at Grazzi's table, glancing at each other nervously. It was the first time they had ever been inside the buildings of Quai des Orfèvres, and it was clear from the expressions on their faces that they had not thought it would be like this. The woman was tall and dark-haired like her sister, but she did not resemble her otherwise. She had been crying. The man looked like a bank clerk, round-shouldered and short-sighted from too much poring over figures. His pale-blue eyes looked timidly out at Grazzi from behind thick-lensed glasses as if he had found himself in a room with some dangerous animal.

He was a book-keeper in one of the Renault branches, not a bank clerk. He let his wife do all the talking, confining himself to an occasional nod of agreement and a glance at Grazzi which seemed to say that was it, that was exactly right.

They had been to the Institute to claim the body of Georgette Thomas. They hoped it would be released to them that night; they had already made all the arrangements for the funeral. They were her only relatives in Paris.

The parents of the two sisters still lived in Fleurac, in the Dordogne. They had a farm there, and a licensed grocery shop–café on the Périgueux road. The sister said Georgette had been, how should she put it, something of the prodigal child of the family. She had come up to Paris when she was only eighteen. She had been going to school in Périgueux at the time of the liberation, and the parties, the dances, and the presence of all the soldiers had turned her head. She was, supposedly, taking a secretarial course, but the family discovered she had been spending more time in the cafés and brasseries downtown than in school. There had been a violent argument at home, and she had wept for days. She wanted to leave, and in the end she had left and come to Paris. Her sister, Jeanne, who was two years younger, had gone to the station with her and put her on the train, believing firmly that she would never see her again.

"And when did you see her again?" Grazzi asked.

Jeanne's face was pale and tear-streaked, and her voice kept breaking in the middle of a sentence. "A few months later, when I got married. I had met my husband the summer before – he was spending his holiday in Fleurac." He nodded vigorously. That was it; that was exactly right.

"And you have lived in Paris since then?" Grazzi said.

"Yes; not far from her, near Place Clichy. But we didn't see each other very often."

"Why not?"

"I don't know. We didn't lead the same sort of life. She was married a year after I was. She worked for a perfume company then, Gerly. She married one of their salesmen, Jacques. He's a good man. She used to come to see us quite often then, Sundays for dinner and sometimes during the week, to go to a movie. And then she was divorced, and we had had our children. Two of them, a boy and a girl. And she didn't come to see us as often any more. She probably thought that we were angry with her because of what she had done, because of the man she was living with – I don't know. But in any case she stopped coming, almost entirely."

"Had you seen her recently?"

"About a month ago was the last time. She invited us to her apartment for tea, on a Sunday afternoon. We only stayed an hour or so; she had to go out somewhere. But she never told us anything about herself any more."

Gabert, seated on the corner of the next table, was still playing with the puzzle. The little metal figures made an annoying, clicking sound as he shifted them about. "Was she the one who wanted the divorce?" he asked.

Jeanne Conte hesitated a moment, looked at Gabert, and then at Grazzi and her husband. She didn't seem to know if she should answer, if this blond young man who didn't look like a policeman had the right to question her.

At last she said, "No, it was Jacques. She had met another man at Gerly, the sales manager, and after a while Jacques realized what was happening. They separated, and she changed jobs. That's when she went to work for Barlin."

"And did she live with her lover after that?"

Jeanne hesitated again. She didn't like to talk about this, especially in front of her husband, who had lowered his head and was pretending not to listen.

"No, not exactly. She had found the apartment on rue Duperré, and she moved in there. I imagine he came to see her, but he didn't live with her."

"Do you know him?"

"We saw him once."

"Did she bring him to your house?"

"No. We met them one day by accident. About three years ago. He had left Gerly by that time too. He was in the car trade. Then a few months after that, there was Bob."

"Who is this Bob?"

"Robert Vatsky. He's a painter, or a musician, or something. I don't really know."

Grazzi looked at his watch, and told Gabert that it was time for him to leave for rue La Fontaine. Gabert nodded and went out, the puzzle in one hand and his scarf in the other. Every time Grazzi saw him go off like this, shuffling his feet, walking like a lazy, unhurried child who would never change his ways, he found himself thinking about Gabert's idiotic first name – Jean-Loup. It always delighted him, just as it did when his son had learned a new word and insisted on mispronouncing it. He didn't know why it should amuse him so, but it did.

"Do you have any idea who could have done this?" he said, returning to the Contes and the matter at hand. "I mean, do you know of any enemies your sister might have had?"

They both shook their heads helplessly, and Jeanne said they didn't know anything about it; they simply couldn't understand it.

Grazzi reached in a drawer, took out the inventory of items found with Georgette Thomas' body, and read off the figures of the amount of money in her handbag, the amount in her bank account, and of her salary. They thought they were perfectly normal.

"Did she have any income besides her salary?" he asked. "Savings? Or any stocks?"

They didn't think so.

"It wouldn't be like her," the woman explained, twisting her handkerchief nervously in her hands. "It's difficult to make anyone else understand. But I lived with her until I was sixteen; we slept in the same bed, I wore all of her clothes, I knew her better than anyone."

She began to cry, silently, compulsively, still looking at Grazzi.

"She was very ambitious. At least – I don't know how to say it – she was capable of working very hard and making all kinds of sacrifices to get the things she wanted. But money itself didn't interest her. She was only interested in the things she owned, the things she had bought with her money. She used to say, 'That's mine; that belongs to me; that's my coat.' Things like that. Do you understand?"

Grazzi said, no, he didn't.

"Well, even when we were children, for instance, everyone thought she was stingy. We used to tease her about it at home because she never wanted to lend me any money from her allowance. But I don't know if stingy was the right word. She didn't save money. She spent it. On herself. She couldn't bear the thought of spending it on anyone else. The only person I ever knew her to buy a present for was my son. She was crazy about him, but even for my little girl it was a different matter. It created some real problems at home; you know how children are. One day we told her so."

"How old is your son?"

"Five. Why?"

Grazzi took out the photographs they had found in Georgette Thomas' handbag, and showed her the ones of the child.

"That's him; that's Paul. Those pictures were taken two years ago."

56

"Then, if I understand you properly," Grazzi said, "you're saying that your sister wasn't in the habit of saving her money, but she was . . . selfish about it. Is that correct?"

"Yes and no. I didn't say she was selfish. In a way, she was very generous, very trusting, with everybody. All the foolish things she did were the result of that. She was very naïve. I argued with her about that. I don't know how to explain it; and now that she's dead . . ."

The tears began to flow again. Grazzi told himself it would be wise to get onto another subject, Bob, for instance, and then to break off the interview and talk to them again, later. For some reason he didn't do it, though; he continued on the same line.

"You argued with her?" he said. "When?"

He was forced to wait until she had dried her eyes with the rolled-up handkerchief and attempted to suppress a nervous hiccuping that made the veins in her neck pulse angrily.

"Two years ago," she said at last. "At Christmas. And for no reason, really; a piece of foolishness."

"What sort of foolishness?"

"The car. She had bought a car, a Dauphine. My husband works for Renault, so she had been to see him several times. He arranged the financing and all the papers for her. She had wanted a car for a long time. For weeks before she even ordered it, she was talking about 'my car'. It was delivered to her on Christmas Eve, and she went straight to a garage and had little initials painted on the front doors. She was supposed to have lunch with us, and she was very late. When she arrived, she explained that it was because she had to wait at the garage. She was so happy; you wouldn't believe it . . ."

Grazzi was finding it hard to look at her any longer. The tears were coursing down her cheeks in a steady stream.

"We teased her about the initials. And then, you know how things like that can happen, you say something you don't really mean, and then something else is said, and before you know it ___. And after all it was her business. But that's what happened. From then on we scarcely saw her at all – five or six times in the last two years."

Grazzi said he understood. He could see Georgette Thomas very clearly, sitting at her sister's table on Christmas Eve, proud of her newly acquired treasure, proud of the initials on the doors, and greeted with sarcasm and derision. The dessert would have been eaten in irritable silence, the parting embraces would have been half-hearted and chilly.

"Well," he said, "robbery doesn't seem to have been the motive for her murder. Can you think of anyone she knew who might have had some grudge against her?"

"No. No one at all."

"You mentioned this Bob person."

Jeanne Conte lifted her shoulders. "Bob is a lazy good-for-nothing, but there are a lot of people like that. I can't imagine him killing anybody. And especially not Georgette."

"What about her husband?"

"Jacques? Why would he want to kill her? He's married again, he has a baby, and besides, he was never really angry with Georgette."

Her husband was nodding approval of every phrase now. Suddenly he opened his mouth wide and announced, very rapidly and in a high-pitched voice, that the crime had undoubtedly been committed by some sadist.

The man in handcuffs at the other end of the room

began to laugh, sitting very straight in his chair, staring down at his manacled wrists. Either he had heard what was said, or he was crazy, or both.

Grazzi got up slowly, and told the Contes that he had their address and would surely see them again before the investigation was completed. As they walked towards the door, nodding to the two inspectors who were watching them leave, Grazzi thought about the apartment on rue Duperré, and asked one final question.

The woman stopped and stared at him, and said no, certainly not, the only person Georgette had been seeing recently was Bob. Georgette was not at all what Grazzi seemed to think she was.

He sat across the table and said that Georgette was an oddball. You had to understand her, and he did. He had never thought for a minute that he was the only man in her life, and jealousy, thank God, was something he didn't even know about. If the inspector was thinking along those lines, he might as well tell him right now that he was off his trolley.

His name really was Bob. That was the name on his identity card. It was Robert that was a nickname. He said his parents had always had crazy ideas like that. They were both drowned in a sailing accident on the Brittany coast when he was ten years old. He was twenty-seven now.

All-right, so Georgette had been thirty when she died. As for his feelings about her death, that was none of the inspector's business. As far as he was concerned, cops belonged in one of two categories: they either disgusted him or they made him want to laugh. He hadn't made up his mind about the inspector yet, but he probably belonged in the second group. Imagining that Georgette had any money was laughable. Imagining that that chicken-livered husband of hers was capable of climbing into a train to murder anyone, that was laughable too. But imagining that he, Bob, had been fool enough to commit a so-called crime of passion – and in a second-class railway carriage, at that – that was sad. He felt sorry for the inspector – what was his name again? – Grazziano, right, he would remember this time – Grazziano couldn't really believe that.

He had come here because it upset him to have the cops still meddling around with Georgette's things. He had been to rue Duperré the night before, and he hadn't liked the mess they had made in the apartment at all, not at all. If you can't put things back where you found them, you shouldn't touch them.

All-right, the inspector could have him locked up if he wanted to, but he was going to say what he came here to say. And if the inspector was all that delicate, it wouldn't do him any harm to listen. If cops were going to be sensitive, they should have thought about it before they chose their profession.

In the first place, Georgette had not been robbed, simply because there was nothing to rob. Even a cop should be able to understand that.

Next, she wasn't the sort of person who would have known – really known – anyone lousy enough to kill her. He hoped that the inspector – God in heaven, what was his name? Grazziano – understood what he meant.

And last, if it was possible to believe the ignorant jargon of an ignorant newspaperman, it had taken three minutes for Georgette to die. He hoped the inspector realized very clearly that this was the worst part of it. Maybe he was the only one who thought about it that way, but every time he did think about those three minutes, he wanted to blow up the whole city. You didn't have to go to night school at the Préfecture de Police to know that those three minutes meant that it wasn't the work of a professional. The son of a something or other who had done it was an amateur. And the worst kind of amateur, at that; not even a talented one.

If he knew how to pray, which he didn't, because he didn't believe in God, he would pray that it had been the work of a professional, in spite of what the newspaper said about evidence. In that case, the newspaperman would just have been filling up his columns with his usual stupidities, and Georgette would have died without suffering.

There was one other thing. When he came in, he had seen the Witch and her Apprentice on the way out. Georgette's sister and brother-in-law – he always called them that. So it was his duty to warn the inspector about them right now, so the cops wouldn't waste any time on the kind of nonsense that used up taxpayers' money. Those two were not to be believed. They were worse than squares, who usually had good intentions at least. Gossips and rumourmongers. Everything they said was as true as the Book of the Apocalypse, which he hadn't read, by the way, but he knew it wasn't true. They didn't even know Georgette. You don't know people you don't love. Whatever they had said, it was just so much hot air.

There; that was all he had to say. He hoped that it had registered with the inspector, who must be bored with having to repeat his name all the time. He was sorry about that, he really was; he never could remember people's names.

Grazzi stared at him glassily, drunk with listening and vaguely astonished with himself for not having called a policeman from the corridor to have this madman carted off to spend a night in jail. He could have talked all he wanted to there.

The man was enormous, a full head taller than Grazzi, and frighteningly thin. The skin of his face was stretched so tight over the bones that his appearance was almost skeletal, and his blue, childlike eyes seemed completely out of place.

Grazzi had imagined Georgette Thomas' lover very differently, but he could no longer remember what he had imagined. This was the reality. He was better than the car salesman, but that was about all that could be said for him. Thinking of the car salesman irritated Grazzi, and this one had given him a headache.

The important thing was that he had been visiting friends in a village about fifty kilometres outside Paris at the time of the murder. Every one of the six hundred inhabitants of the town could confirm this: he was not the type to pass unnoticed.

Gabert telephoned at quarter past twelve. He was in a *tabac* on rue La Fontaine, and had just left the Garaudy apartment. He had seen the daughter-in-law, and he had to admit it, she was damned good-looking.

"She doesn't know anything; didn't notice anything at all, can't tell us anything at all."

"Do her descriptions agree with the ones Cabourg gave us?"

"She didn't describe anything. She says she went to bed as soon as she got on the train, and went straight to sleep. She hardly remembers the murdered woman. She got off the train as soon as it pulled in, because her mother-in-law was waiting for her."

"She must have noticed something about the other passengers . . . and besides, it doesn't tie in with what Cabourg said. He told me the berth on the upper left was still empty at eleven-thirty or twelve."

"He might have been wrong."

"I'm waiting for him now; I'll see. What's the woman like?"

"Pretty. Dark hair, very long, big blue eyes, saucy little nose, about five foot six; just right. She's upset about the whole thing, there's no doubt about that. She talks backwards; you know the type. All she wants is to be left out of it. She'll come in and make a statement tomorrow."

"Didn't she notice anything at all during the trip?"

"Zero. She says she'll be no use to us at all. She got on the train, went to bed, went to sleep, got off, and her mother-in-law was waiting. That's all. She doesn't know anyone, didn't notice anything."

"Is she just stupid?"

"She doesn't seem to be. She's just upset. You can see that she doesn't like being mixed up in this sort of thing – the family, and all that . . ."

"All-right. We'll talk about it this afternoon."

"What should I do now? I have a friend who lives near here; I could have lunch with her."

"Go ahead. After that, go out to Clichy and see the truck driver, Rivolani. I'm going to wait for Cabourg a little longer. We'll go to see the actress later this afternoon."

At three o'clock Commissioner Tarquin was sitting at the desk in his office, typing up a report. He was still wearing his overcoat, and he seemed pleased with himself. Tarquin was very good at making out reports; he knew all the right words, and used them.

He looked up as Grazzi came in, and said, "Hello, Mr. Holmes, how goes it?" He didn't look him in the face, though, just at the knot in his tie.

Grazzi stood in front of the desk, waiting until the boss had finished. He typed with both hands, like a real typist. Grazzi himself was so clumsy with a typewriter that he made rough drafts of everything in longhand, and even after that he made mistakes.

The boss said everything was working all-right. He leaned back in his chair, took a badly crushed cigarette from his pocket and straightened it between his fingers. Then, as usual, he asked for a light; someone was always stealing his matches. He puffed contentedly for a moment, and said the boys upstairs were going to get this slot-machine business dumped right in their laps in just three days; Wednesday morning. He would see the big boss himself, and after that they would see what would happen.

And how were things going for Grazzi? He had been thinking about this murdered woman this morning in his bath, and he had some advice for him. All Grazzi had to do was keep his ears open.

He stood up and began pacing about the room dramatically, the way he always did, and said, right, there wasn't anything so complicated about all this. First, she was strangled because of something that happened before she went to Marseille. Second, because of something that happened while she was there. Third, because of something that happened after she left, in the train itself. The important thing was to establish the motive.

Grazzi murmured something about oversimplification,

but the boss said, tut, tut, tut, if you can reach a solution without a motive, let me know, I'm not that bright myself.

He said that Grazzi, who was an intelligent man, had certainly recognized that two of the three hypotheses were no good. The first and the second. If the so-and-so who did this had known the woman before getting on the train, there wasn't a chance in ten thousand that he would have chosen that particular place or time to go and choke her to death. Even if he was completely cracked, he would have preferred the middle of Place de la Concorde or an exhibition at the Grand Palais: he was much less likely to be noticed there, if you know what I mean.

Tarquin stopped his pacing, took his hands from his overcoat pockets, and planted a nicotine-stained index finger on Grazzi's tie, staring at it fixedly.

"No! It's in the train that everything happened, Mister Holmes! It's that night you have to know everything about. From ten-thirty on Friday night to seven-fifty on Saturday morning; that's the beginning and the end of it."

He tapped the finger emphatically against Grazzi's chest, punctuating his words. Unity of time, unity of place, unity of anything you can think of; it's classic. If she was throttled in the train, it's because the person who did it didn't know her, and wasn't in a position to choose a better place. Whoever it was, he (or she) was in a hurry; it had to be done then and there.

He touched the finger against his own temple, and nodded, "Believe me, I know what I'm talking about. You just keep that in mind. Now, is there anything new?"

Grazzi said, no, nothing very much, he had questioned some people, but none of them had been anywhere near the station at the time of the murder. They still had to check on the whereabouts of the ex-husband, Jacques Lange, and also a student who lived in the building on rue Duperré and had known the murdered woman. He was waiting for a report from Marseille.

"And the other passengers in the compartment?"

"Cabourg didn't come in this morning. But he probably told me everything he knew over the telephone. We've found three of the others, an actress, a truck driver, and the wife of some electronics engineer. Gabert saw her this morning, and is seeing the truck driver now. We'll get to the actress later."

'Who else is there?"

"The berth opposite the Thomas woman, No. 223. If Cabourg is right, it's a young girl who got on at Avignon. Her name is Bombat. We haven't had any luck finding her; she isn't in the directory here."

"And what about Thomas herself?"

Grazzi said, nothing more just yet, but he was beginning to know about her. Even as he said it he was frightened, because he knew it wasn't true, he had never really known anyone. It was going along just the way it always did: statements, faces, theories, and nothing at the end of it but the smug self-assurance of this fat, opportunistic man who would never look you in the face, who was sitting back at his desk again now, putting his hands back in his pockets.

Grazzi found a note from Gabert on his table. The report from Marseille had been telephoned in, and would be brought to him at about four o'clock. An inspector down there, a Corsican whom Grazzi knew, had retraced all of Georgette Thomas' movements in the four days preceding her death. Nothing.

He leaned against the window behind his table, looking out at the Seine, wondering if Tarquin was right. A boat moved down the river, rowed by twelve men in red sweat-shirts breathing twelve little clouds of fog.

Gabert brought the report in himself. Six typewritten pages, in triplicate. He had been out to Clichy before he came back to the Quai, and had seen Rivolani, his wife, and their children. Nice people. They had given him a cup of coffee and a glass of Armagnac. They had talked about everything, even the murder.

"Oh, shut up," Grazzi said, "and read this yourself. After that, we'll go and see the actress. Then to Cabourg's; he never showed up here."

They both sat down to read. Gabert was chewing gum, but for once he had put the puzzle aside.

Georgette Thomas had arrived in Marseille at 8:37 A.M. on Tuesday 1 October. At about nine o'clock a taxi had dropped her at the Hôtel des Messageries, rue Félix Pyat, in the Saint-Mauront district of the city. She had stayed at the same hotel on previous visits to the city. It was in a working-class neighbourhood inhabited primarily by Italians, or families of Italian origin.

From that time until her departure on the night of Friday 4 October, her days were completely taken up by her work as a special demonstrator in a downtown beauty salon called Jacqueline d'Ars, in rue de Rome. She always left the salon at about seven o'clock, and spent all of her nights, including the first one, with a man named Pierre Becchi, a steward on the Compagnie Générale Transatlantique liner *Ville d'Orléans*.

Description of Pierre Becchi: tall, dark-haired, usually

very well dressed, heavy-set, thirty-five years old. Police record: two terms in the naval prison at Toulon during his military service, for disorderly conduct; nothing since then. Due to sail on the *Ville d'Orléans* at the beginning of November, on a ten-week trip to the Far East. He had met Georgette Thomas the preceding February, during one of her earlier trips to Marseille. At that time he had stayed with her, in her room at the Hôtel des Messageries. Until her arrival in October, he had not seen her again, or had any word from her.

During the afternoon of Tuesday 1 October, Georgette Thomas had made a call from Jacqueline d'Ars to a bar in rue Félix Pyat where Pierre Becchi spent most of his time ashore. Since he was not there when she called, she had asked the proprietor, Monsieur Lambrot, to tell him she would be there that evening at about eight o'clock.

At about eight o'clock Georgette Thomas had met Pierre Becchi in the bar, where he was playing cards with some friends while he waited for her. They had dinner together at a nearby pizzeria on Boulevard National, and returned to the Hôtel des Messageries together at about ten.

On the following days Georgette Thomas had met her lover in the same bar at the same time, and they had had dinner in the same pizzeria, except for Thursday night, when they had gone to a movie and had supper afterwards in a restaurant in the Old Port.

In the mornings, she always left the Hôtel des Messageries first, took a bus at the corner of rue Félix Pyat and Boulevard National, and went straight to work. She had lunch with the employees of Jacqueline d'Ars, in a cafeteria on rue de Rome. Pierre Becchi did not leave the hotel until towards the end of the morning.

None of the people questioned in the first few hours of the investigation had noticed anything unusual in the murdered woman's behaviour or attitude.

Pierre Becchi had been questioned on Sunday morning, but was unable to furnish any information of importance. He had only known Georgette Thomas for a total of about ten days – five in February, four in October – knew nothing of her life in Paris, did not know about any possible enemies or any motive for the murder. Friday night, having had a quick dinner with her at the pizzeria, he had taken Georgette Thomas to Gare Saint-Charles. He had left her at the gate to the platform, about two minutes before the scheduled departure of the train. At the time she was strangled in Paris the next morning, he was in Marseille. All of this could be confirmed.

The Marseille police were continuing their investigation. If there were any new developments, further reports would be sent in immediately.

The weather in Marseille the first four days of October had been beautiful. The Corsican inspector who phoned in the report said that it still was.

Before leaving Quai des Orfèvres with Gabert, Grazzi went back to Commissioner Tarquin's office to give him a copy of the report from Marseille. The boss had gone, so he put the typewritten papers on his desk, and as he did so he glimpsed a scrawled memorandum beginning with his name:

Grazzi. If everything happened in the train, it's robbery. In any case, it's some kind of nut.

Grazzi's first thought was that there were lots of definitions for some kind of nut, but Tarquin's peremptory statements always influenced his thinking, and he knew it. He read the memo again and shrugged: there was nothing to steal.

Gabert was waiting for him on the staircase, listening to the complaints of three inspectors from another office. His hands were deep in the pockets of his duffel coat, and he was chewing gum, but he was following everything they said with such obsequious attention that Grazzi suspected he was pulling their legs.

They were leaning against the wall of the landing just above Jean-Loup, counting off the number of nights since they had slept. For an entire week they had been running around Paris, trying to find some boy who had either run away from home or been kidnapped, or something. But just this morning they had been taken off that, and all three of them had been assigned to a murder that had taken place the night before: some character who had got himself shot in the gents at the Central boxing arena, talk about a place for a murder.

Until Saturday morning both Gabert and Grazzi had been working on the hunt for the boy too, because he was the son of one of the town councillors of Nice. The police of ten *départements* were looking for him, and in Paris all the airports and stations and the known hiding places of Saint-Germain-des-Près, Montparnasse and Montmartre were swarming with police.

Gabert nodded when he saw Grazzi approaching, and said, they were right, it was a rotten deal, but what could you do about it? Then they left, Grazzi first and Gabert following, shaking his head in sympathetic understanding.

In the little Renault 4CV, with Grazzi driving, Jean-Loup took out the inevitable puzzle. They took the *quais* on the Left Bank, in the direction of Place de l'Alma.

"What do you think about it?" Grazzi said.

"About what?"

"The report from Marseille."

Without taking his eyes from the puzzle, Gabert said you really had to go and see for yourself; reports don't tell you anything, they just gossip.

"But after all," Grazzi said, "we've got to trust them. If they didn't find anything, it's because there was nothing to find. The boss thinks it all happened in the train."

In two succinct phrases Gabert made it clear what he thought of the boss, and what he could do with his ideas. They entered the tunnel opposite the Tuileries, and when they came out there was a red light. Grazzi took out his handkerchief.

"Can you understand that, a guy who sees a girl every six months for four nights," he blew his nose, "and then they kiss each other goodbye," he blew his nose again, "and say *ciao* until the next time."

Jean-Loup said, yes, he understood it all-right, there wasn't anything very complicated about it. Grazzi put his handkerchief away and wiped his nose with the back of his hand. He said he had never met a woman like that.

"Like that, or any other kind, for that matter. I haven't met very many at all. I was married when I was twenty."

Jean-Loup said, "Don't tell me the story of your life, the light's green." They started off again. The sky above the Seine around Place de la Concorde was low and grey, and there were wisps of fog floating above the river.

"When did you tell them to come in, Rivolani and the other one?"

"Tomorrow morning," Gabert said, "but we won't get

anything out of it. The girl doesn't know anything, and he doesn't know much."

"Does he remember the other people in the compartment?"

"Vaguely. He says he slept all the way. He didn't pay any attention to anything. But his descriptions agree with Cabourg's, except for the upper berth on his side, Garaudy. He didn't see her either, but he doesn't know if she was already in the berth when he went to sleep, or if she came in later. That could confirm what she says, or what Cabourg says; take your choice."

"What about her; what's she like?"

"She doesn't look like a woman who goes around strangling perfect strangers."

Grazzi said that Georgette Thomas didn't look like a woman who met a man every six months for a few nights, and never gave him a thought in between. But she was.

"You don't know that she never gave him a thought in between," Jean-Loup said. "The world's gone around a lot of times since you were twenty, chief; you'd better set your watch right."

It was five o'clock when they closed the doors of the car, in a no-parking zone in front of the building where Eliane Darrès lived. The street was narrow and quiet. At the end of it they could see a corner of the Palais de Chaillot, a pale-yellow triangle against the sky.

The apartment building was a good one, with a thick-carpeted staircase and a lift that worked.

"That's a piece of luck," Grazzi said.

He felt tired, a weariness that started in his head from too much thinking. He couldn't put himself inside this poor girl's skin, he didn't understand her; there was no point in even trying. Question people, take notes, be a workhorse, and go home to your family at night, that's all you can do. If the case drags on too long, they'll bring in some more workhorses. Sooner or later they would drag up something, they would uncover whatever it was they needed.

As the lift rose, swiftly, silently, he looked at Gabert, who was not looking at him, and was probably thinking about something else altogether – a girlfriend or something like that, but certainly not the case. Grazzi envied him his withdrawn air, the tranquil look around his eyes and mouth. Jean-Loup would never be a workhorse, he had no desire to uncover anything, he didn't give a damn about promotions or the opinions of his superiors. He had come into the police force three or four years earlier because, he said, his father was a nut on the subject of public service, a pigheaded maniac, and the only way he could get any peace was to do as he said. His father must be something or other in one of the ministries, perhaps the Interior, and if that was true, he could push his son along from behind the scenes.

As they got out of the lift on the third floor, Gabert said he hoped this wouldn't take long. He had a date to meet someone on the Champs-Elysées at eight o'clock, and if they had to see Cabourg after this he would never get there on time.

They rang the doorbell, and while they waited for it to be answered, he buttoned his duffel coat carefully and ran the palm of his hand over the wave in his hair.

"What's she like?" Grazzi asked.

"Who?"

"Your date tonight."

Jean-Loup said, bah, just as stupid as the rest of them, and then the door opened.

Eliane Darrès was wearing a pink dressing gown, and pink slippers trimmed with white fur. Grazzi had not thought he knew her, because the name meant nothing to him, but he recognized her immediately. He had seen her in a dozen or more films, always in small parts, and always the same kind of parts. She must have had very little to say in them, because her voice surprised him.

It was a high-pitched, affected voice with an irritating quality of playfulness; the voice of a woman who has nothing much to occupy her days, and no maid to open the door, but feels compelled to say that she has an appointment in ten minutes, and it's impossible to keep servants these days.

She led them through a pink corridor into a pink room. The lamps, standing on little round tables, were all lit. She had long, dyed hair, rolled into a heavy chignon at the back of her neck. When she turned around and gestured for them to sit down, her oval face and great dark eyes were those of a woman of forty-five who seems older, because she is trying too hard to look younger.

Berth 222

Eliane Darrès almost lost one of her slippers as she led the two men into the living room, and because of that, she didn't have time to hide the bad chair. The glue was gone on one of the legs, and it squeaked terribly; she was always afraid it was going to collapse.

The inspector who had told her his name was Gracino or Graciano sat down in it and unbuttoned his overcoat. His companion, the young one, went over and sat down on the sofa, looking bored and taking some kind of game from his pocket.

She heard the first protesting groans from the chair and the little metallic clicking of the puzzle at the same time. The little blond inspector didn't even seem to have noticed her.

She knew his type, only too well. They walked into your house as if it were their own, sat down and crossed their legs, and let you bring them a drink, without even saying thank you. Usually they were students of something-or-other, the law or Oriental languages or something like that, and they went on being students for years on end. They were calm, pretty, rude, and played at being strong, silent types; they attracted women without even looking at them, they made love to you once and made you lose your head, and then they started talking about how hard they had to study, that was the only thing that really counted, but everything would be different after their exams. Sometimes they kissed you, very quickly, with warm, indifferent lips, like children, or put a hand on your knee when you came back from the beauty parlour and said something nice about how you looked, but that was all there was to it; they were enough to drive you crazy.

This one wasn't a student, he was an inspector, but he didn't look like one. He never lifted his eyes from the game in his hand, and the speed with which he moved the little disks from one place to another was both annoying and fascinating, like a television screen you don't want to watch, but it's there and you can't help it.

"We won't keep you very long," the one named Graciano said. "We've already talked to three of the other passengers in your compartment. Unfortunately, their stories don't entirely agree, but that's perfectly understandable. The first thing you think about on a train at night is sleeping, so you don't always notice the same details."

She said that was true enough, and sat down on the good chair facing him, arranging the folds of her dressing gown carefully over her knees.

"I see you're wearing a wedding ring," he said. He was a tall man with a thin, bony face. "Are you married?"

"I was. I lost my husband several years ago."

He took a little red notebook from the pocket of his overcoat, opened it to a page where he had put a pencil as a marker, and began taking notes, just the way they did in films. He asked if it would be indiscreet to get some personal questions out of the way first, so they would know something about her.

He wrote down that she was an actress, had been a widow for eight years, that her real name was Dartetidès, that she was forty-seven years old, and that she had just spent a week in Aix-en-Provence, where she had been making a film.

She hoped for a minute that he wouldn't ask her if she had returned to Paris as soon as her work in the picture was completed, but he did. She knew that he could check on everything she said easily enough, so she confessed that they had only needed her for three afternoons, and she had stayed in Marseille a few days longer in the hope of finding work on another film. She said all actresses did that, even the stars, trying to kill two birds with one stone.

There was a moment's silence, and then the tall, thin inspector said he understood.

"You reserved your berth, No. 222, on Thursday 3 October; is that right?"

'Yes. It was the lower one on the right-hand side. There were two other passengers in the compartment when I got on the train."

Marseille. The streets of Marseille at ten o'clock at night. The little café on Boulevard d'Athènes, at the foot of the great staircase of Gare Saint-Charles, where she had had tea and some sweet biscuits. The noise and the lights in the station. The weight of her suitcase.

When she entered the compartment, at almost the same time as the man in the leather jacket, the other one was putting his baggage in the rack, and had climbed up on her berth without taking off his shoes. She hadn't dared say anything about it, though; she never did. And after that, he had helped her lift her own suitcase to the rack.

She had been annoyed that there were men in the

compartment. She had even thought vaguely of changing to a berth in first class, wondering how much it would cost. She kept hoping that there would be other women, at least; but no one came. She could see herself now, sitting sideways on the berth, leaning forwards because there was very little room above her head, pretending to be looking for something in her handbag, waiting for the train to leave, for all the nonsense of goodbyes to end, and for the corridors to empty out.

"Then the victim didn't arrive in the compartment until after you did?" the tall inspector said.

"I still can't think of her as the victim. Yes, she came in just before the train left. Another woman – a young girl, really – got on during the night, at Avignon."

The night before, at Chez André, after the telephone call from the police, she had gone back to the table where her friends had already started on their dessert. They had been stunned when she told them what had happened, and one of the men had gone out into rue François Ier, to get a copy of *France-Soir*. There were seven or eight of them, and they had spread the paper across the table so they could all see it. People at neighbouring tables had stopped eating to watch and listen.

"The victim was a dark-haired woman, wearing a dark suit," Gracino or Graciano said.

"Yes. I saw the picture in the paper last night, and I recognized her straight away. It's terrible, in fact, how clearly I could see her again. I couldn't stop thinking about it all night."

"Had you ever met her before seeing her in the train? Her name is Georgette Thomas."

"No, never."

"Are you sure of that?"

"Absolutely. She had the berth just above mine, you know."

"Did you speak to her?"

"Yes. You know – the kind of conversation you have with people you meet on a train. She told me that she lived in Paris, and that she was in the perfume business. She recognized the one I wear, and we talked about that for a few minutes."

"Was this just after the train left?"

"No, later."

"Try to tell us everything you can remember about the trip, from the minute you first went into the compartment." She nodded and glanced at the other inspector, the blond one, who had not spoken, not even looked at her. She wondered if she should offer them a cup of coffee or a glass of port, or if it was against the rules for them to accept anything like that while they were on duty.

"When I went into the compartment, there were two men already there. One of them had the upper berth on the right, two above mine. He looked like some sort of government clerk, very serious . . . I don't know why I say that, really; he just made me think of a government clerk. Maybe because of his suit; it was old, and shabby-looking . . . I don't know."

She was saying the wrong things again. And she couldn't help staring at the dark-blue overcoat on the inspector seated across from her; it was too tight for him, and worn at the elbows. He was a government clerk, too; at least, a sort of government clerk. He wasn't writing in the little notebook any longer. He was watching her, listening to her while she said the wrong things.

She knew what she should say, though. She had scarcely slept the night before; and all morning, in the kitchen, she had been thinking about the trip and preparing the phrases she would need to describe it.

"There's one important thing," she said abruptly. "He had an argument with her."

The little metallic clicking stopped. She turned around and met the indifferent, but vaguely curious, eyes of the blond boy.

"Who? The clerk?" he asked.

"His name is Cabourg," the other inspector said. "What do you mean by 'had an argument with her'? Did he know the victim?"

She said no, she hadn't had that impression.

"I don't exactly know when it was, I was reading a magazine, but she wanted to take down her suitcase to get something out of it. It was the one who looked like a clerk, this Cabourg, who helped her with it. After that they talked for a while in the corridor, like two people who have just met. I don't think they knew each other, because I heard the beginning of the conversation, and it didn't sound as if they did. It's hard to explain."

The tall inspector nodded. "I understand," he said. "Then it was later that they argued? What about?"

He was looking at her thoughtfully, and she didn't answer right away. He had very clear, watchful eyes, and a pale, troubled face. She said that it wasn't too difficult to guess. That sort of thing must often happen on trains.

She knew that the blond young man was watching her too, and she sensed that he was probably amused. He had undoubtedly guessed the reason for the argument even before she said anything, and he thought that she was glad it had happened, that she was jealous of the dark-haired woman. Let him think whatever he liked.

"I don't know," she said. "After he had talked with her for a while in the corridor, maybe he said something, or did something . . . At least, that's what I thought happened. Before they left the compartment, he had been watching her in a funny sort of way. It's something women notice, but another man might not. In any case, they had an argument. She was the one doing the talking, and she sounded angry. The door of the compartment was closed, and I didn't hear what she said, but you couldn't mistake the tone of her voice. She came back in a minute later, alone, and went to bed. He didn't come in until much later."

"Approximately what time was it then?"

"I don't know. I looked at the time when I went to the toilet to change for the night, and it was eleven-thirty then. The argument was probably about an hour later."

"Do you remember whether it was before, or after, the conductors came through for the tickets?"

"It was after, I'm sure of that. By that time there was another woman in the compartment. The one who got on at Avignon. A young blonde girl, quite pretty, wearing a blue coat and a light-coloured dress. She must have been reading, because hers was the only light that was lit when the conductors opened the door and asked for our tickets. You know, they have those little electric bulbs above each berth."

"Then it was after midnight?"

"Absolutely."

"What happened after that?"

"Nothing. She went to bed. Later, I heard the man come in and climb up to his berth. The other man, the one who had the berth on the lower left opposite mine, had turned his light out a long time before. Then I went to sleep myself."

"You don't remember anything else about this argument?"

"No; I think I've told you everything."

"Would you think that Cabourg was angry with her?"

She remembered the way the man in the shabby suit had looked the morning before, when they arrived. His face was pale and haggard, his eyes had refused to return her greeting, and when he paused on the threshold of the compartment to excuse himself for disturbing her, his voice had been a submissive whisper. She said no, she didn't think he was angry. The metallic clicking had started again.

"He left as soon as the train got in," she said, "without speaking to her, or even looking at her. You could tell that he was embarrassed, and wanted to get away from us as quickly as possible."

"And what about her?"

"That was different. She wasn't embarrassed at all, and she didn't seem to be in any hurry. She just hadn't thought about it again, or at least she was trying to give that impression. She talked to me, and to the girl from Avignon. The man in the leather jacket left next, and said goodbye. I think that was the first time he had said anything since he had said good evening the night before."

"Cabourg left first, then. And after him the other man, Rivolani. Is that right?"

Eliane Darrès shook her head, and said no, Cabourg hadn't left first, not until after the young man in the other upper berth. The metallic clicking stopped abruptly, the blond boy lifted his head, and the tall inspector tapped his pencil thoughtfully against his lips.

"A young man?" he said. "Which berth are you talking about?"

"The upper one, on the left-hand side. The young man . . ."

"What young man?"

She couldn't understand what it was she had said that made them react like this. The blond one was staring at her with no expression at all in his eyes, and the other one looked openly incredulous. For a minute or two he didn't say anything, and then he explained to her that they had located the occupant of the upper berth on the left. It was a woman named Evelyne Garaudy. The whole time he was talking, he studied her with a kind of irritated concentration, as if he were disappointed in her. He was thinking that she was mistaken, and therefore she could have been mistaken about everything else; her testimony could not be trusted. An unemployed actress, getting on in years, and probably just wanting to talk to get herself in the spotlight.

She shook her head stubbornly, and the inspector sighed.

"What did this young man look like?" he demanded.

"Quite tall, and thin, I should think. To tell you the truth, I never really saw him."

There was a short, insolent, whistling sound from the young inspector in the duffel coat, and the other one looked up at the ceiling and shrugged. She went on talking to him, because she knew that if she turned to the other one she would blush and act like a fool.

"Look, Mister Gracino, you don't seem to believe me, but I know __"

"Grazziano," the inspector said.

"Excuse me – Mister Grazziano. When I say that I didn't see him, it's because he came into the compartment very late, after all the lights were out. And he didn't light one to go to bed."

"You said that you were sleeping too."

It was the blond one who said that, so she had to turn to him now. He wasn't looking at her, he had taken up the silly puzzle again. She hated him, she could have hit him, would have liked to hit him. He had the same pretty mouth they all had, like a crafty child's, and if she were to kiss him she knew exactly how it would be, because she knew them all too well. All their kisses were alike.

"I was sleeping," she said, and she could not prevent her voice from cracking a trifle, "but he must have stumbled in the dark – there wasn't much room, with all the baggage on the floor . . . That woke me up."

She thought: I know what I'm saying, I know what I know, he almost fell on me as he passed; I can recognize that kind in a crowd, I can see them in the dark; they have warm, indifferent lips, like children, they are children, they're wicked and they're wonderful. I can recognize them, I hate them.

"It was a woman," the other one said. (Grazziano – if I use the wrong name again, he'll know that I was mistaken; he'll think I'm crazy.)

She shook her head, not knowing what words to use, thinking: I am not mistaken, I didn't see him, but I know. He was exactly like all the rest of them, like your little friend who doesn't look like an inspector, like the student in the café on Place Danton a year ago. Calm, indifferent, with something about them that drives you mad, to be so

84

young, to have skin so clear, to walk into a compartment on a train and wake up everyone, and stumble over everyone, without even saying excuse me, just like that. He didn't say excuse me, he said God damn it, what have I done now, and he almost fell on top of me. He must be tall and thin and awkward, the way they all are. Then he climbed into the berth on the other side, and he must have fallen on the girl from Avignon, because he laughed, and she laughed too. Just like that, in the darkness on a train, at one or two o'clock in the morning.

"I heard his voice," she said. "After he got to bed, he talked for a long time to the girl in the berth below his. I'm certain it was a boy, a very young boy. I don't know how to explain it to you, but I know . . ."

The one whose name was Grazziano got up and closed his notebook, leaving the pencil between the pages. Why did he carry the notebook? He had written down almost nothing. Standing in front of her, he was even taller than she had thought, and bonier; an enormous carcass in a worn overcoat, with a pale, troubled face.

"One of the other witnesses — Cabourg, to be precise — also heard that conversation, but he says it was a woman's voice. You could be mistaken about that."

His voice was tired; he seemed less interested in convincing her than in putting an end to the matter, and getting on to something else.

"In any case, we have already located her."

She shook her head again, glanced at the blond one because she knew he was not looking at her, and said, perhaps, I don't know, but I certainly thought it was a boy. And even while she said it, she was thinking, I am not mistaken, I can't be mistaken, a woman doesn't say God damn it when she stumbles over you and wakes you up; there must be some way I can explain it to them.

But to do that, she would have had to explain so many other things, so she said nothing, and just went on looking up at the inspector with the bony face, shaking her head stubbornly. She could see the corridor again just before the train left, crowded with passengers; and the blond, unhappy-looking boy who was standing near the entrance to the compartment, and had moved aside to let her in. It couldn't have been the same one, but that blond boy, with very black eyes, in a grey tweed suit, was somehow linked in her mind with the incident later that night, with the voice from the upper berth whispering to the girl from Avignon. She had laughed at whatever it was he said; a little, muffed sound that was as annoying as the clicking of the game in the hands of the blond inspector.

"When you woke up in the morning," Grazziano was saying, "the occupant of that upper berth wasn't in the compartment?"

She said no, but the movement of her head said no, I am not mistaken, I could explain it to you, but I would have to tell you about a boy who put his hand on my knee when I came back from the beauty parlour, and kissed me the very first time we met, in a café on Place Danton. I would have to tell you about things that hurt too much, things you would think were sordid, and I can't do it.

"I didn't see anyone," she said. "I went to the toilet to dress at about six or seven o'clock, I'm not sure. But I do know that when I came back, the berth was empty. The woman who was murdered was still in her berth; she smiled at me and said good morning while I was putting my pyjamas and dressing gown in my suitcase. The girl from Avignon was putting on her dress – she must have taken it off in the dark. I remember that, because we joked about it. She was having trouble trying to get it on, stretched on her back in the berth. In the end she got up and put it on, and said it doesn't matter, the men are asleep anyway."

The man in the leather jacket had still been snoring loudly, his face looking drawn and twisted with fatigue. She had noticed his hands, and thought he must be a dock worker or a mechanic, something like that. His suitcase was sitting upright on the berth, at his feet; a faded-blue pasteboard affair with battered corners. Cabourg wasn't moving, but she had been sure he wasn't asleep, and she had thought, he's probably watching the girl get dressed, and the little bitch undoubtedly knows it. Ugly things she had been thinking, and untrue, like all ugly things. The poor man wasn't thinking about the girl at all, she had known that as soon as he got down from his berth and she saw his face, and the haunted look in his eyes.

Grazziano was speaking to her again. "Did someone come to meet you at the station?"

"No. Why?"

"No reason."

He put the red notebook in the pocket of his overcoat. He really was terribly tall. She went on looking up at him and said, "If you'll let me say something that is just my own impression, I'm sure that none of the people I saw in that compartment could have done this terrible thing. It's just an instinct, but I'm quite sure of it . . ."

The inspector nodded briefly, looking a trifle annoyed, said thank you, and glanced over at the blond one, who stood up, his mind on something else, his eyes on something else, putting his scarf around his neck and tucking the ends inside the duffel coat.

She followed them to the door, and the tall one, Grazziano, said, "Could you come to Quai des Orfèvres tomorrow?"

She said yes, and he asked her to be there at ten o'clock, room 303, third floor. He said she might remember some other details before then; that he was going to think about everything she had said and that she could make a statement. And then they were gone, and she closed the door behind them, leaning against it, with her hands locked on the knob, hurt, and angry with herself.

Three minutes later, the bell rang again. She had gone back to the living room, and because to sit in the same chair would have brought back the feeling of deceit, she hadn't had the courage to do it, and had stretched out on the sofa instead, with her arm thrown across her eyes. She knew as soon as the bell rang that it was the little inspector, the blond one. She didn't know why he had come back, but when she got up to answer, her hand touched the puzzle, lying on the sofa beside her. He had forgotten it.

A little metal square, like an abacus, with thirty-six numbers, black on red. You shook them up, then rearranged them in proper order – a plaything.

She almost lost the slipper again as she walked across the hall, pausing to glance at herself in the convex surface of the witches' mirror. The distorted image that came back to her was that of a teacher she had had at school twenty-five years before: dark eyes, much too large, a hairless forehead, and a nose that went on for ever. It occurred to her that it was almost the face of Cabourg.

The blond inspector in the duffel coat with the neatly

folded scarf had a beautiful, impertinent smile, the same smile they all have when they need you. He said he had forgotten something and came in, without even saying thank you or excuse me.

She closed the door and followed him into the living room. He walked straight to the sofa and bent over it, looking for the silly game.

"I have it," she said.

She held out the metal square, keeping her fingers closed around it. He walked over to her, and since she didn't give it to him, but held her arms tightly against her breast, he just looked at her calmly, with that innocence they all pretend to have, and said I'm sorry, I forgot it. He held out his hand, and she heard herself saying to herself: I've got to give it to him, he's a police inspector, you are mad. She thrust his hand aside with a stupid smile, she knew it was stupid, and then, abruptly, she gave him his silly game. She felt his hand against hers, it was warm, and he went on looking at her, the same indifferent look, not even smiling.

"There's also one question we forgot to ask," he said.

She had to move back a little, because he was standing too close, putting the metal square in his pocket. He wasn't much taller than she.

"When you left the compartment, was the victim getting ready to leave?"

"I don't know. I guess so, yes. I said goodbye to both of them, to her and the girl from Avignon. I think they were getting ready to leave."

"Were there many people in the corridors?"

It was curious, his voice was high-pitched, almost shrill; not like the voice of the other inspector, who must be waiting for him downstairs in the car.

"There were a few people, yes. But I waited until most of them had gone; I hate crowds."

"And you didn't notice anything as you left that might have something to do with the murder?"

"No, I don't think so."

She said she would think about it now, she hadn't paid much attention. After all, she couldn't have known that someone would strangle a woman in the compartment she had just left, and a young inspector would come and ask her what had happened.

He smiled, said of course she couldn't, and walked in front of her towards the door. He stopped in front of the witches' mirror, hanging on the wall in the hall, looked at himself, and said that's funny, you really look like hell in these things.

He patted a hand against the pocket where he had put the silly game and said that he always forgot everything, everywhere he went. He asked her if she did the same thing.

"No, I don't think so," she said.

He tilted his head to the side, lifted his shoulders, and said, well, perhaps I'll see you tomorrow, if I'm there when you come in.

"I don't think I was very helpful to you just now," she said.

He said, oh, yes, she had been. He opened the door himself.

"Everything you told us about Cabourg, about the argument, we didn't know that. We're going to see him now; we'll find out whether he's trying to hide anything."

"Do you suspect him?"

"Who," he said, "me? I don't suspect anyone. To tell you the truth, I'm a very bad cop; I hate suspecting people. I'd rather condemn them all. There's no such thing as an innocent man. Do you believe in innocence – really believe in it?"

She laughed stupidly, knowing that this boy thought she was stupid, that he was saying anything that came into his head; he was making fun of her.

"Do you think it's innocent," he said, "to help someone take down her suitcase, when what you have in mind is making a pass at her later, in the corridor of a train?"

He shook his head with that sulky smile she knew so well, and said, as a matter of fact, why had she been taking down the suitcase?

"What was it she was looking for?"

She tried to remember, she could see the dark-haired woman reaching up, and her skirt above her knees as she put a foot on the berth, and the way Cabourg had looked at her.

"Aspirin, I think, or some sleeping pills. I think it was aspirin."

He said well, it probably didn't matter, but in any case no one is innocent, or at least if you are you have to be very young, after that the whole thing is rotten.

She held herself very straight in the doorway, with her arms at her side, like an idiot before the cameras for the first time. He left her standing there, lifting his hand a little, very briefly, to say goodbye and she didn't even think about going back or closing the door until after he had left. She watched him go down – he walked, he didn't take the lift – and her eyes must have looked like the eyes of a kitchen maid you picked up at a dance hall; she was a fool.

She had dinner at the kitchen table, with a book open in front of her, propped against the bottle of mineral water, reading the same page over and over again, unable to rid herself of the thought of the murdered woman.

Long black hair, deep-blue eyes, tall and slender in her well-cut suit. A smile that lit her features suddenly, surprising you with its warmth and intensity. Georgette Thomas had smiled often during the trip. When she came into the compartment, she had smiled and apologized for disturbing them. She had refused a lozenge when it was offered to her, smiling and saying, thank you, you're very kind. She had even offered a cigarette to Cabourg, smiling and saying, please, help yourself. And in the morning she had smiled at the forty-seven-year-old woman who was cold and had slept badly and was thinking of returning to solitary dinners at the kitchen table, with a book propped against a bottle of mineral water, and said, good morning, we seem to have arrived.

The poor woman didn't know that she was going to die; it had never occurred to her that she was arriving for the last time. I should have said that to the inspectors, I should have told them that.

The newspaper they had all read the night before in the restaurant had said that it wasn't robbery, but what could it have been? What had she thought about in those minutes while she was dying? What do you think about while someone is killing you?

Eliane Darrès got up from the table and did the dishes: one plate, one glass, one knife and fork, and the pan in which she had cooked the eggs. Then she stood for a long while in the corridor between her bedroom and the door to the apartment, hesitating between the idea of sleep and anything else at all; anything would be better than staying here alone.

She said to herself, I still have time to go to a movie. She went to one of the cinemas in the neighbourhood almost every night, telling everyone that she did it because, after all, it was her profession and she had to keep up with what was being made, but that she hated it, and had a terrible time trying to find the necessary two hours. Sometimes she saw the same films again, because she had no memory for titles, and the photographs in the foyers were all lies. It didn't matter though. Anything at all was better than staying here. She always bought mints during the interval. Anything at all.

Surveying her reflection in the mirror on her dressing table the next morning, she was pleased to see that she looked rested and fresh. It was a beautiful day, with a warm sun shining over the Trocadéro. As she dressed, she looked out through the windows at the calm blue sky, and made up her mind that she would be calm.

A woman she did not know had been murdered; it was sad, but that was all. There was nothing she could do about it. She would tell them what she knew, and would not concern herself with what they thought of her.

In the first place, she was not mistaken, she *could* not be mistaken, about the boy in the upper berth. Whatever bearing it had on the murder was something they would have to find out for themselves, but the voice she had heard, the presence she had felt in the darkness, was that of a boy, not a woman. If they did not want to believe her, that was up to them.

She would also try to explain to them that Georgette Thomas had had no reason to be afraid; that she certainly had not suspected she was going to be murdered. If the girl from Avignon had been strangled, it would have been just as unexpected, just as unbelievable. It would be difficult to explain a way of smiling, but she would have to try; it was important.

She wondered if she should attempt to describe the way Cabourg had looked when Georgette Thomas put her foot on the lower berth and reached up for her suitcase, and the movement had lifted her skirt above her knee. If she did, and the blond inspector was there, he would make that insolent, whistling sound again. He would be thinking that he knew what kind of woman she was, that she saw evil everywhere she looked, because that was the way she thought herself.

What was the stupid thing he had said? That no one is innocent; everyone is guilty.

The mistake she always made was to worry too much about what other people thought of her. She knew what it was they thought, and she also knew that they were wrong. A woman clinging to a vanished youth, trying to buy it back. The pain and wretchedness that they called sin. The spectres of approaching age; the demons of the afternoon. She had been married for twenty years, to a man she had never once deceived. He had always been ill, and there were times when it seemed that the picture on the chest in her bedroom was scarcely less real than he had been in life.

Opening a drawer of the chest to take out her gloves and handbag, she stood for a moment looking at the photograph. He had been gassed in 1914. He was kind and gentle, the only human being she had ever known with whom she was unafraid, and at the end he had been in such pain that she had watched him die with a feeling of relief.

Sin. She had had two lovers, one before her marriage, during the holidays of the year she was eighteen; and the other just last year, long after her husband's death. And she still did not understand how it could have happened, either time.

She had no memory of the first one at all; could not recall whether he was handsome or ugly, or even his name. She could remember nothing except her fear that someone might come in. Even now, when anyone talked about the young girls she knew and the things they did, she felt ill at ease – not because she felt she had done something terribly wrong, but simply because she couldn't remember it. That little idiot of eighteen had been someone else; it could not have been her.

In the hall, as she went out, she caught a glimpse of herself in the witches' mirror and thought of the teacher at school, and of the little idiot, and of the woman, almost thirty years later, who had let herself be kissed in a bistro on Place Danton by a boy she had never seen before.

It was strange when you thought about it: at an interval of thirty years, she had had two lovers of the same age, almost as though they were the same one, as though the first one had not grown old while she had. He had probably been preparing for his exams, too, and spending his time in the same sort of bistro, playing billiards, in just the way that this one played the slot machines.

The lift stopped between two floors, and she had to push all of the buttons, both up and down, before it started again. At last it did, but stopped again almost immediately. It's some imbecile, she thought, or a practical joker upstairs, he's got the door open, I'll have to call the concierge. She didn't like the concierge; he never said good morning or good evening, and his clothes were always dirty.

She pushed the button for the top floor, the fifth, and the lift started up, but stopped again just below the fourth. She didn't understand it, and tried the other buttons again.

It was weird that she should have been thinking of Eric, just when this happened. One night when he was waiting for her on the landing, he had done the same thing: he had seen her coming up in the open cage of the lift, and opened the door on her floor. She had tried all of the buttons, while he opened and closed the door, forcing her to go up and down until at last she had called out for the concierge. Just as a joke, because he was twenty years old, or nineteen, because he had a sullen, pretty mouth, as they all have, because they're enough to drive you mad, and they know it.

She had wept when she finally got out of the lift, and he had said, what about me, I was furious, waiting for you all this time. It was true that he had been waiting; she had given him a key the next day, and on some nights after that she had found him sleeping on the floor in the living room, stretched out like a cat, with his hands behind his neck. Now it's really stalled; I'll have to call the concierge.

For five or six weeks, perhaps two months, Eric had been there almost every night, and after that, there had been times when she went to look for him in the café on Place Danton – she hadn't wanted to, but she couldn't help it. He owed her money, and that was a reasonable pretext for looking for him, for hoping, for anything at all that was better than a movie and little mints in the interval; what do you think about while someone is killing you?

She was still pressing on the buttons, had not even lifted

her head, the year-old memory had not even caused her to look up, when the certainty came to her that she was going to be killed, when she thought, he's standing up there above me, watching me; there's no roof on the lift cage, he's looking down at me, and laughing.

She lifted her head towards the floor above, very close to her, just as the gun went off and the bullet tossed her like a puppet against the wooden wall of the lift, thinking it's impossible, it can't be true; her neck and shoulders slammed against the wooden wall, someone standing above me, just like Eric, I can recognize them even in the darkness, all their kisses are alike, the whispering and the laughter, like the boy in the upper berth and the girl from Avignon, like the hand on my knee when I came back from the beauty parlour, that same little idiot again, lying against the wall in the lift, in the darkness.

Berth 221

Ernest Georges Jacques Rivolani, independent trucker, born 17 October 1915 at Meaux (Seine-et-Marne), residing at No. 3, Impasse Villoux, Clichy (Seine), had been killed by a bullet from a Smith and Wesson .45 fired into the back of his neck at point-blank range at about 11:00 P.M. exactly eleven days before his birthday, for which his wife had bought him a pair of fur-lined driving boots. In addition to his wife, he left three children, of whom the youngest was a boy of thirteen.

He was stretched face-down on the cement floor beneath the open suspension door of the rented garage where he kept his car, wearing his Sunday suit, with his left arm beneath his body and his right arm flung out above his head. He had been shot before he could put the car in the garage; it was still standing in the middle of the court – a 1952 Citroën 11, whose motor had finally stalled.

"It's lousy," Mallet said.

He hadn't slept at all the night before, because they had called him at one o'clock in the morning, and he kept shaking his head, fingering the stubble of beard on his chin, his eyes glassy with fatigue. On Sunday, while Grazzi and Gabert had gone from Rivolani to the actress and from the actress to Cabourg, he had journeyed from one end of Paris to the other with the murdered woman's address book in his pocket, questioning everyone he could find.

Grazzi, who had never had a telephone installed at home, because it cost thirty-five thousand francs he didn't have, had slept from eleven o'clock until eight-fifteen. He was freshly shaved, wearing a clean shirt, and feeling vaguely guilty. Tarquin had not arrived and Grazzi was sure he knew why; he was getting panicky, and wanted to stop by the office first and talk to someone higher up. He was a good cop, but first things first, let's keep ourselves covered, if you see what I mean.

"It's a lousy business," Mallet repeated, shaking his head, "but you didn't have to see the wife. She was hysterical at first, but now that the children are there, she doesn't say anything, she just looks at you as if you could give her back her husband. When she opens her mouth at all, it's to talk about those boots – I couldn't stand it any longer. She bought them for his birthday, and it's all she thinks about: he was cold in the truck. I swear to you, it's true."

Grazzi nodded, looking at the body on the floor, thinking I should never have let myself get involved in a case like this, I should have learned twenty years ago not to take on more than I can carry. And Tarquin still isn't here.

Rivolani had been thrown forward, crushed like a paper doll by the weight of the bullet. His body was a full yard forwards of where he must have been standing. The shot had been fired from directly behind him, so close that half of his head had been blown off, and there was blood splashed across the back wall of the garage.

A policeman was taking measurements. Grazzi turned away and walked back towards the Citroën. Mallet followed him, as if attached by a magnet; Grazzi could smell the cheap brilliantine he used in a futile effort to hold down a mass of hair as thick and wiry as his beard.

There were ten concrete-block garages in the group, facing each other across a cement square about twelve feet wide. They all had overhead doors, secured by padlocks. Rivolani's house was at the end of the street on the corner of the *Impasse*, a little blind alley with no pavement, just a scattering of grass.

The night before, the truck driver had gone to the cinema with his wife and youngest son, just as he always did on Sunday nights when he was not on a trip. The boy would not be going to school today.

'What time did they get back?" Grazzi asked.

'Eleven o'clock, eleven-fifteen. They went into the city, to a cinema near Saint-Lazare. Rivolani wanted to take them to see something cheerful, because of what had happened on the train. He dropped them at the door of the house, and then came here to put the car away. His wife says he only used it on Sundays, to take them to the country, or to see a film. When he hadn't come back about an hour later, she began to get worried. The boy was asleep, so she came out here to see what had happened, thinking he must have had some trouble with the car. She screamed, and woke up the neighbours and they called the Commissariat in Clichy."

Grazzi looked at the interior of the car, noting how clean and well kept it was. In his spare time Rivolani had probably taken his son to the garage with him, and together they had cleaned the Citroën and talked about cars and motors, the father sure of himself and the son sure of his father, just as Grazzi would do with Dino later, when Dino was older and they had a car.

"And nobody heard anything?" he said.

"Nothing," Mallet answered. "Not until the wife started screaming. The worst thing is that she turned out the headlights; she remembers turning out the headlights. Can you imagine that?"

Wait and see, Grazzi told himself, just wait and see; he's going to break down completely and start bawling, and Tarquin will arrive at exactly the same moment, and take it all out on me.

But Mallet was accustomed to not sleeping, and he didn't break down, he just kept shaking his head and staring around him without seeing anything. Then the boss arrived at last, braking hard just beside the Citroën, alone in his black Peugeot with the steel hook at the back. When he went on holiday, he towed a little boat on a trailer.

Tarquin gestured vaguely to Grazzi and Mallet, and walked over to the open door of the garage, without pausing to speak to them. They could see him bending over the corpse, and the policemen and deputies from the Commissariat in Clichy pausing in their work to watch him. Thirty seconds later he straightened up and walked back into the unexpected sunlight of this October Monday. There was a note of relief in his voice, and what he had to say was the first sensible thing that had been said that morning:

"A gun like that, there's a record somewhere. There aren't too many crooks with .45s in the first place, and any son of a bitch who works his shells like that one is a pro. But he's pulled a first-class boner here. If you know many of them who go around signing their jobs with a cross, then you know them better than I do!"

* * *

The bullet had been carefully grooved with two lines that intersected across its snub nose, and then the lines had been ground down with a file, so that it would burst into four jagged pieces on impact. In the laboratory, Rotrou, who had spent thirty years of his life studying bits of lead, talked about a cartridge which fragmented after penetrating its target, tearing it to pieces. According to him, they had been used in the Far East during the last war. He also remembered a fairly recent trial at Fort-Lamy in French West Africa; some professional hunters had been accused of using them to kill animals. He would be able to tell them more about it later.

In the meantime there were five of them gathered in the boss's office: Grazzi, Jouy, Bezard, who had brought Georgette Thomas' suitcase with him, Alloyau, and Pardi, the Corsican, who was leaning against the door, smoking. Mallet had been sent home to get some rest. Gabert was checking the employment agencies and all of the neighbourhood Commissariats, trying to locate the girl from Avignon.

Tarquin's round face was gleaming with sweat, and a half-smoked cigarette hung listlessly in his mouth, extinct and forgotten. He was taking Mallet's place himself, and Grazzi reflected that he even looked like him. He shook his head continually, and stared at the men around him without appearing to see anything; for once, he hadn't been able to find anyone to assume responsibility. He was cursing quietly, steadily, saying damn it, why did they always have to louse things up the minute his back was turned? What the hell had Grazzi been doing since Saturday morning?

"Saturday was the day before yesterday," Grazzi said,

"and yesterday was Sunday. Did it occur to you on Saturday that someone was going to eliminate this guy?"

"What do you mean, eliminate?"

"I just said it because that's the way it looks to me."

Pardi stirred restlessly in his corner and said the word was well chosen; someone had undoubtedly eliminated the truck driver, because he had been a witness to something. Pardi's voice was soft and musical, and he spoke very slowly. For some reason this always impressed them, and they listened to him carefully. There was a moment's silence in the room now, because what he had said was what they all thought.

"Had he been questioned?" Tarquin asked, in a distinctly calmer tone.

"Yes – yesterday afternoon. I sent Gabert to see him. He was supposed to come here this morning to make a statement."

Grazzi got out the red notebook and found the page where he had written down what Jean-Loup had told him about the interview. When they had come back from Cabourg's the night before, they had sat down at one of the tables in the deserted inspectors' room and gone over all of this. Cabourg had not been at home, but they had looked at his apartment anyway. They didn't have a warrant, and the concierge had been difficult, so they had just glanced around, not touching anything. When they had talked about it later, they were more concerned about Cabourg and the reasons for his absence than they were about the truck driver. And Jean-Loup had been in a hurry to get away; he was already late. There were just a few scattered words on the page marked "Rivolani" – not enough to fill three lines of a report.

"He made a regular weekly trip to the South, carrying odd lots of merchandise on the way down and fruits and vegetables coming back. Last week his truck broke down on the way down, near Berre, and he had to leave it to be repaired. It was going to take several days, so he decided to come back by train. He was going down again at the end of the week to pick up the truck."

Tarquin pushed his hat further back on his head, and said, "All-right, all-right, I didn't ask for the story of his life."

"So he took the train Friday night. The descriptions he gave of the other passengers agree with those of Cabourg and the actress. We went to see her yesterday afternoon too. She should be in the waiting room right now."

Grazzi looked at his watch: eleven-thirty. She might have got tired of waiting by this time. Without taking his eyes from the knot in Grazzi's tie, Tarquin told Jouy to go and look, and send the woman in right away. If she had left, they would have to get her back.

Grazzi went on with the meagre account in the notebook. "Rivolani said that, with his kind of work, he went to sleep as soon as he sat down anywhere, except in the truck. In the compartment, he was the first one to lie down and the last one to wake up. He didn't see anything, and he didn't hear anything."

The musical voice behind Grazzi said he must have seen or heard something; they hadn't been waiting for him when he came home from the movies just to punish him for having slept too long.

"In any case," Grazzi said, "he didn't remember anything. The murderer probably has a better memory than he did."

The telephone rang briefly; a call from one of the other offices. Tarquin picked up the receiver, nodded, said yes several times, thanks old man, and hung up. Grazzi was in luck: he had one thing to go on, at least – the revolver.

"Rotrou is categorical. It's a Smith and Wesson, recent model, unquestionably contraband, and someone who knows about guns. There was a silencer. Rotrou says it's a pear-shaped affair, not a standard-cylinder type; he says he can draw a picture of it."

Tarquin's use of words like "categorical" annoyed Grazzi to such an extent that it sometimes blinded him to facts. He said it wasn't the first time Rotrou had guessed the colour of a murderer's eyes from the shape of a piece of lead and been proved wrong, so as far as drawing pictures goes, don't make me laugh.

The boss stood up, so suddenly that it looked as if he planned to swallow the burned-out cigarette, and Grazzi with it. He didn't say anything, though. He pushed his hat forward on his head, clasped his hands behind his back, and turned away from them, staring out of the window.

Grazzi's heavy, cold-thickened voice went on relentlessly, saying if you want my opinion, we'd better get moving, we haven't found this Cabourg yet, he left his apartment in such a hurry that he left one of the lights burning, and if we wait too long, he'll have some more work for the undertakers. He paused for a minute, and then said, he had a wife and three children, Rivolani.

Tarquin said it's a hell of a world.

He was standing motionless in front of the window, looking worried, almost human. One of the seams in his overcoat had been torn for several days, and he didn't seem to have noticed it. He was probably thinking it isn't

Cabourg, it's a pro. If I could put ten men to work on the gunsmiths and run a few informers through the mill, I'd know who it was in forty-eight hours. I could pick him up, hand him over to that pighead Frégard, and this imbecile Grazzi could go on playing Sherlock Holmes, if it amuses him. Who does he think he's talking to?

The telephone rang again, an outside call this time. Tarquin turned around slowly, picked it up, listened for a minute and said what the hell? – Where? – In a lift? – then put a flabby hand over the receiver, and said damn it, Grazzi was right about one thing, they'd better get moving, all of them, because now they were all in it up to their necks; they could stop worrying about the actress waiting outside, she'd been shot two hours ago. Then he went back to the telephone, said okay, okay, we'll be there, who do you think you're talking to?

They had put her on the bed in her own room. In order to leave the lift where it was when they found her, they had had to carry her down one floor. One of her high-heeled shoes had fallen off, and someone had stood it in the corridor, just inside the door.

Eliane Darrès' face still registered her final astonishment. The bullet had smashed her chest like a blow from a hammer, but there was not much blood, except on her dress and her leopardskin coat.

Jean-Loup arrived, breathless, while Tarquin and Grazzi were still standing in front of the bed, staring down at the body. He said good morning, chief, looked down, and then abruptly turned away, his face twisted, as if he were going to vomit. Grazzi took him by the arm and led him out to the landing by the lift and the staircase.

He was very frightened now.

On a Saturday morning, in a compartment of a train, someone kills Georgette Thomas, for some reason, to settle something. Saturday night, one newspaper has the story, with a simple list of names, and on Monday the others appear, mentioning Cabourg, Garaudy, Darrès, Rivolani. And because something has gone wrong with the murderer's plan, and this something is important, two of the other passengers in the compartment have been killed.

Grazzi thought of Cabourg, gone since Saturday night, leaving a light on in his room. Murderer or already murdered?

Grazzi thought of the girl from Avignon, whom Gabert had not been able to find. The murderer seemed to be cleverer or better informed than the police; had he been able to find her?

"They killed Rivolani too?" Gabert demanded.

"The same way she was killed. From less than two feet, with a gun like a cannon. Why do you say 'they'?"

"I don't know," Gabert said.

He was very pale, but seemed to be all-right now. Twenty-three years old. A profession he must really hate this morning. Grazzi hated it too, standing with his hand on the grille of the lift door, thinking: "they" found Rivolani Sunday night, before there was anything but his name in the paper; maybe they found Cabourg too. And the Bombat girl?

"Did you find out anything about the girl from Avignon?"

"Nothing in the hotels. I've covered almost all the Commissariats, and I've got to do the agencies this afternoon. But it takes time, you know, if I'm alone. Whoever it is, he's faster than I am."

Gabert said it very softly, his throat tight and hoarse, motioning towards the open cage of the lift. Grazzi was thinking: this is it, right now, I always knew it would happen some day, Tarquin will go off with his boat for a couple of years, he can afford it, and he'll get back when the ministers change; but I'll end up a clerk in some provincial Commissariat, unless I have some courage and get out altogether, into insurance, or one of the department stores, it doesn't matter. It was as simple as that; there was a madman loose who was faster than they were.

"It was clever, his trick with the lift," Grazzi said wearily.

He took Jean-Loup by the arm again and led him up to the fifth floor, just above the empty cage.

"She gets into the lift on her floor. He lets her go down, and then he opens this door. How he knew it was her, I don't know. Maybe he watched for her first, from the staircase just above her floor – and that leopardskin coat is easy to recognize. He keeps opening and closing this door, while she tries all the buttons. If she comes up, as he wants her to, he closes it. If she starts to go down, he opens it and stops her. See? He brings her up to the fourth floor with no trouble; he can stop her anywhere he likes."

Grazzi closed the door and aimed two fingers through the open grillework, repeating that it was very clever, this was a clever bastard.

"But why didn't she call for help?" Gabert said.

"That's the cleverest part of it. You call for the concierge if the lift doesn't work. But it was working. It wouldn't go down, it went up, but that was all. She probably just thought she'd get out at another floor and walk down."

They heard Tarquin's voice on the landing beneath them, talking loudly to the policemen and some of the tenants in the building. They walked back down.

The boss looked at Grazzi's tie, with his hands in the pockets of his overcoat, his hat pushed back on his head, and said, yes or no, Mr. Holmes, does this son of a bitch have a silencer?

"He has one," Grazzi admitted, "but where is it going to get us to concentrate on that? Before we could check all the gunsmiths and the licences, or dig up some informer, he would have had all the time he needs to use his silencer! And besides, the sort of thing Rotrou said it was, he could have made it himself."

"He'd need equipment, all kinds of machinery."

"There are dozens of guns found every day that aren't licensed or registered."

"But not silencers."

"Do you think it could be a political setup?"

"Not a chance," Tarquin snorted. "I make up a report like that and send it to the boys upstairs, and I'd have it back on my desk tomorrow. And before it was over, I'd be retired."

"Maybe it's a foreigner?"

"Oh, sure," Tarquin said. "Czechoslovakian, for instance; they have good guns. Don't get that idea in your head; it isn't the boys at Orly who'll have to take off their uniforms and go fishing – it's us!"

He shook his head gloomily, said he would see them later, and started down the steps.

The telephone was on a table beside the bed where they had put Eliane Darrès. While Grazzi dialled a number,

Gabert began searching the room, carefully averting his eyes from the figure on the bed.

When Mallet answered the phone, his first words were simple obscenities, but he had slept for a full hour and recovered some of his normal good humour: all-right, he would shave and dress, get back to the office, and sit on the line to Marseille, keep them working. He understood.

Jouy was at the Quai, waiting for Grazzi's call. He had been questioning Madame Garaudy, who had been in the waiting room when he went to look for Eliane Darrès. But all he had learned was that she was pretty, well dressed, seemed to be frightened, and holding something back. She didn't remember anything, didn't know anything, wanted to sign her statement and get out as fast as possible.

"How long ago did she leave?" Grazzi asked.

"About a half an hour."

"Does she know about Rivolani and the actress?"

"No."

"Well, find her, and stay with her."

"Why?"

"If you don't know, there's no point in explaining to you. Just stay with her; don't let her out of your sight. I don't want to find her with a hole in her head."

"Why can't we just put some policemen around her house?"

"Perfect," Grazzi said. "Why don't we put an ad in the newspapers? I want to catch this bastard, not make him run!"

"Speaking of newspapers, there's a whole gang of vultures outside. What shall I tell them?"

Grazzi looked at his watch. "It's twelve minutes past twelve," he said. "If they have anything to publish tonight that they don't know already, you're the one who's going to have a hole in their head."

He hung up.

Pardi was next on his list; he was having lunch at home. He had no phone, and took his calls on one belonging to a neighbour who had long since regretted his generosity. Pardi answered with his mouth full, his normally soft voice sounding thick.

"I want Cabourg," Grazzi said.

"I only take orders from the boss," Pardi mumbled.

"Well, this is an order."

"What's going on?"

"What do you think?"

"Oh, all-right, all-right," Pardi said, and hung up.

Grazzi was sure that he would find Cabourg. He did his work calmly, quietly, without any fuss, and with the firm intention of becoming, one day, director general of the Sûreté. He always found what he was looking for, because he was Corsican and he had friends everywhere; and he was the only man who worked for Tarquin who knew how to arrange things so he could have lunch at home.

Alloyau was not to be found anywhere. He was undoubtedly having a steak in a cheap restaurant in rue Dauphine, with his bottles of pills lined up on the oilcloth table cover, telling the waitress about his troubles with his digestion. He would return to the Quai at exactly two o'clock, straight and thin as an i, looking very pale and very English, smoking the one cigarette he allowed himself every day.

Grazzi left instructions for him with the clerk at the office. "Tell him to bring in, this afternoon, Madame Rivolani and any relatives there are of Cabourg and Darrès, and question them. Tell him to get that car salesman and

Georgette Thomas' sister back, and question them again. And tell him to find Georgette Thomas' husband and that Bob Vatsky, and have them come in tonight, so I can talk to them. I'll call back about two o'clock."

"What shall I do?" Gabert asked. He was not wearing the duffel coat today; he had on a navy-blue raincoat of shiny nylon, and a bright-red tie.

"We'll go and get some lunch at Place Clichy," Grazzi said, "and after that you can take the car while I go to see that student who lives upstairs in rue Duperré. I want you to find the Bombat girl; you've got to find her."

Jean-Loup nodded, but he looked very uncertain.

They ate a *choucroute garnie*, sitting by the windows of a large brasserie, looking out at the play of light and shadow in Place Clichy. They had had lunch in the same place on a very hot day two months before, when they were working on another case in the area. It had taken them eight days, and it was Tarquin who had finally solved it.

Grazzi was thinking of the truck driver, the fur-lined boots, and the short last walk he had taken from the car to the garage to open the padlock, lift the door, and then nothing. He hadn't heard the killer come up behind him, his body had been hurled forwards by the impact of the bullet, and his wife had come and turned out the headlights.

"Can you think of anything that could have unnerved the bastard to that extent?" he asked Gabert. "What could Rivolani have known, so that he had to kill him too?"

Gabert shook his head, swallowed, and said, after all, if Rivolani had noticed anything, he would have told him about it, he had questioned him himself.

"But that's just it," Grazzi said irritably. "He may have seen something without paying any attention, because it didn't mean anything to him, but it would to us! Why do you think two people who happen to have been in that same compartment have been killed in two days?"

Gabert shook his head again, said he didn't know, he had no idea, finished his glass of beer, and took half of what was left in Grazzi's glass.

"He's upstairs, in his room," the concierge had said, "but I hope you won't have to ask him too many questions. He's terribly upset."

He was tall; dark-haired, about twenty years old, a good-looking boy with fair skin and an unruly lock of hair falling across his forehead. He called himself Eric Grandin, but in looking through his papers, Grazzi saw that his first name was really Charles. He smoked Gitanes, never stopping, lighting one from the other with long, restless fingers. He was very thin, and the blue V-necked pullover he wore, with no shirt beneath it, seemed far too large for him.

The room was very small, and littered with books. There was a little butane heater standing on a table, surrounded by notebooks and pages of texts. He had been lighting it when Grazzi rang.

"I was making some Nescafé," he said. "Would you like some?"

He handed Grazzi his coffee in a cup, and poured his own into a glass that still bore traces of wine at the bottom. He was wearing a gold watch, the same way Jean-Loup wore his, with the face on the inside.

"Georgette gave it to me," he said. "I know what you're going to ask, so I might as well tell you right away: yes,

113

I was her lover, I loved her very much and she loved me; and on Saturday morning, at the time it happened, I was here, getting ready to go to a lecture. The concierge can testify to that; she brought my things up."

She had already testified to it. The things were his milk, some bread, and two shirts she had laundered for him – she always did his shirts, and probably for nothing.

"I don't know anything about it; I can't understand it. I didn't even learn about it until I read the paper that night, at a friend's house in Massy-Palaiseau. I had Georgette's car; I still have it. I just don't understand it."

His face was drawn and pale, there were real tears in his eyes, and when he turned aside to light another cigarette his adolescent fingers trembled.

Grazzi drank his coffee standing up, looking around him. Phrases that made no sense at all, formed from words cut out of magazines and newspapers, were pasted together everywhere, hanging on the walls. And side by side with them were photographs of every conceivable domestic animal, staring out at him with great, gentle eyes.

"I'm studying to be a vet," the boy explained. "Third year."

It was research he was interested in. One day he would have a farm in Normandy, a sort of laboratory–clinic where he would breed splendid animals with eyes like those. Either that, or he would go to Australia or South Africa, somewhere where there were still great open spaces, and animals of course. Men didn't interest him. That was all rotten; they had made a botch of everything.

"How long had you known her?" Grazzi asked.

"Two years. I met her when I first took this room, two years ago."

"And have you been her lover all that time?"

"No, not until about six months ago. But I went down to her apartment all the time, we had dinner together and talked."

"Do you know Bob Vatsky?"

"He's the one who found this room for me. I met him in a bar, the Quartier. He plays the saxophone. But if you think he did this, you're wrong."

Grazzi saw no reason to tell this boy that Vatsky had a better alibi than his. He just nodded and said, "When you met him, was he already her lover?"

"Yes."

"And you knew it?"

"Yes, I knew it."

"In other words," Grazzi said slowly, "you were both her lovers at the same time?"

For an instant the boy looked startled, and then, when the point of the question dawned on him, he laughed. He said Georgette wasn't the only one, he had quite a few other friends.

"And some nights," Grazzi said, "when you went down to her apartment, he was there too?"

"Of course. What of it?"

"And neither one of you was jealous?"

He laughed again, a sharp, mirthless sound, lifting his shoulders contemptuously, because he understood what Grazzi was driving at and thought it was idiotic.

"If you think she was killed by a jealous lover," he said, "you can save yourself a lot of time by looking for him somewhere else."

His voice rose, unexpectedly, so that he was almost shouting, good God, Georgette was free to be in love with anyone she liked. Not only was he not jealous and neither was Bob, but the three of them often had dinner together, and for that matter he could tell the inspector a few other things, but there wasn't any point because he certainly wouldn't understand them either.

Grazzi was not sure whether he was exaggerating his anger in an attempt to conceal his nervousness, or whether it really did stem from some emotion he could not understand.

"Becchi," he said, "Pierre Becchi – did you know him?"

"Who?"

"A steward on a ship, Pierre Becchi . . . Never mind. Did you ever, at any time, hear Georgette Thomas mention an actress named Eliane Darrès?"

He said no, never, lit another Gitane from the butt of the old one, and mashed out the butt in a plastic coaster that served as an ashtray.

"Or a truck driver named Rivolani? Try to remember. Rivolani. It's important, if you want to help us find out who killed her."

The boy closed his eyes and waved a hand in front of his face to scatter the clouds of smoke from his cigarette. He thought for a minute, then shook his head and said no, he couldn't remember that name, he didn't know anything about it.

"You said that on Saturday night you were at some girl's house, in Massy-Palaiseau . . ."

"A woman, not a girl. She's married and has three children; it's not what you think."

"Then you hadn't planned to see Georgette Thomas that day?"

"I didn't even know she was coming back. She didn't tell me everything, you know. Sometimes we didn't see each other for a week or more, because I came in late or she was away somewhere, working. When she wanted the car, she left a note under my door, and I left the keys and the licence with the concierge."

He was half sitting on the work table, the cigarette between two fingers already stained with nicotine, at twenty, looking straight at Grazzi, an unruly lock of hair falling across his forehead. Uncertain, determined to brazen it out.

I'm wasting time, Grazzi thought, and left.

The rooms on the top floor had once been servants' rooms, and the lift ran only as far as the floor below. Grazzi started down the staircase, thinking about a fifty-year-old widow who had turned out the headlights without knowing what she was doing, and a young woman with a pleasant smile having dinner with two friends and kissing them both good night. He suddenly felt older, more tired than ever.

He passed a boy in a raincoat going up to the top-floor rooms, as blond as the other one was dark, but even younger, looking solemn and thoughtful, reminding him vaguely of a face he knew. He had probably seen him in the building the day before yesterday.

"Are you a friend of Grandin's?" he asked.

The boy stopped, blushed violently, and said no without seeming to understand.

Grazzi nodded and walked down to the lift on the next landing, thinking of himself at seventeen, at twenty.

He telephoned the Quai from a café in Place Blanche. Alloyau had called in Madame Rivolani, Bob Vatsky, Georgette Thomas' ex-husband, and Cabourg's sister. He was expecting Madame Rivolani at any minute and the others were all coming later in the afternoon. Cabourg's sister lived in Créteil, and she was going to have to bring her children with her because she had no one to leave them with. She hadn't even known that her brother had gone to Marseille.

"Where is Mallet?" Grazzi asked.

"On another line, talking to Marseille. They rang about half an hour ago with something rather odd, a statement by the maid in the hotel. You know, the Hôtel des Messageries. Mallet wants to talk to the maid himself; he seems to think it might be important."

"What was it?"

"I'd have to transfer you to him. I don't know myself."

"Never mind, I'll be there in a few minutes. You didn't find anyone to question about the actress?"

"I have some addresses that were found in her apartment. Producers, actors, no relatives. The ones I've talked to didn't know her very well. They didn't say so, but she must have been a pest."

It was three-fifteen when he arrived at the Quai. He forgot to get a receipt from the taxi driver; he would have to pay it himself.

Alloyau was questioning Madame Rivolani when he opened the door of the inspectors' room, but there was nothing Grazzi could tell her yet, so he did not go over. She was wearing a red coat, which she would have dyed black tomorrow; she was sitting very straight in her chair, holding a corner of her handkerchief clenched between her teeth. Alloyau was concentrating furiously on the typewriter, not daring to look her in the face.

Mallet was at the table, leaning over a jumble of hand-written notes. His eyes were red with fatigue when he looked up at Grazzi.

"Wednesday night, when Georgette Thomas and the steward returned to the hotel at eleven o'clock, the maid heard them talking on the staircase. Her name is Sandra Leï. I talked to her myself, because I wanted to be sure to get the exact words. She says it was approximately this." He picked up one of the pages of notes. "Georgette Thomas said, 'No, it's nothing. Don't pay any attention to me. And besides, I'm not sure.' They were going up to the room, they passed Sandra Leï on the staircase, and they didn't say anything more. That's all. The maid says she thought at the time that it was very strange, because Georgette Thomas didn't speak to her and didn't even seem to see her. She says that the Thomas woman was very polite, and always spoke to her."

"What did she think about it?" Grazzi said.

"Well, what she remembers particularly is the words, 'And besides, I'm not sure.' She's certain that those were the exact words. She thought that Georgette Thomas might be pregnant, and was worried about it."

"That's absurd. It would have come out at the autopsy."

'Thomas might have thought she was. We don't have any way of knowing. In any case, I told Marseille to send someone to talk to the steward again. They're going to call back."

Tarquin thought it was absurd, too, but that Georgette Thomas might have been mistaken and thought she was pregnant. After all, she had said she wasn't sure.

He was sitting at his desk, in his shirt sleeves, with his hat still on his head, and on the desk in front of him Grazzi saw a pile of files from the Criminal Records Office and the General Intelligence Division, files containing details of thefts and disappearances of weapons. Tarquin saw Grazzi's look and said, there's no need to fly off the handle, I asked for them this morning, I was just looking through them to see. He said he hadn't realized himself how guns could be passed around like that, or just disappear completely.

"They even pinch them from us. In February they rounded up some character who had lifted his from a recruit in the Saint-Sulpice Commissariat. He was taking it home with him to clean, and it's a good thing it wasn't loaded, or he might have had one of his own bullets in his head, instead of just being hit with a lead pipe."

He tapped the open files with the flat of his hand, and said, the things you can learn from these, it's crazy; what have you been doing?

Grazzi sat down in the armchair opposite him, unbuttoned his overcoat, and told him about Eric Grandin.

"You can learn from them, too," Tarquin said. "You'll have to come and talk to mine, one Saturday. He's going on twenty-two, and I've never seen any more sign of a brain in him than the day I heard him say goo-goo in the Saint-Antoine Maternity. I hope you do better with yours."

"We were the same way," Grazzi said.

"You think so? Did you have the money to smoke Gitanes, one after the other? Did you spend all your time drawing pictures in the Beaux-Arts, or dreaming about a farm in Australia? Did you used to share your girl friend, after dinner, with a buddy who played the saxophone? We were the same way with one hell of a difference, my poor friend: we didn't live on the same planet."

* * *

At three-fifty Mallet was talking to Marseille on the telephone again. Pierre Becchi didn't remember the conversation on Wednesday night, said that Georgette Thomas had her ups and downs like everyone else, and he hadn't paid any attention.

But whether he remembered or not wasn't important any longer, as a matter of fact, because the Corsican inspector who was at the other end of the line, the same one who had phoned in the first report, had another piece of information. He passed it on to Mallet with a worried note in his voice that made his accent even harder to understand than usual; he wasn't sure whether these Paris people would say thank you or tell him he was an idiot.

Mallet himself wasn't sure whether it was simply the fatigue of three days without sleep or the feeling of having at last come across something really important, but he felt dizzy. He said, thanks, old man, put down the telephone, and sat perfectly still for a long moment, pinching the bridge of his nose between his eyes. Seven hundred thousand francs! The price of an inexpensive car. Do people kill for seven hundred thousand francs?

He got up, walked over to the door, paused there and turned to Alloyau, who was alone now, holding a telephone against his ear, and said, Georges, Georges, don't bother about it any more, let it go, I think we've got it.

He went into the boss's office, found Grazzi and Tarquin there, said excuse me, I may be going to say something stupid, but the Thomas woman, the actress and the truck driver, do you think they were worth two hundred and fifty thousand apiece?

"Last week, in that bar in Marseille, the one that Becchi always went to, they sold a ticket on the National Lottery.

It won seven hundred thousand francs. That's not the big prize, but what do you think?"

The boss leaned back and smiled, a smile that was almost terrifying, because all it reflected was self-satisfaction. Grazzi's brain didn't function quite so rapidly, and for a second or two, he just stared at Mallet. Then he leaped to his feet, reaching for the telephone.

Tarquin had the receiver in his hand already, telling the switchboard to get him the offices of the National Lottery, anyone there, it didn't matter, but hurry; and then two calls to Marseille, the Préfecture there, and a bar in rue something or other (Félix Pyat, Grazzi told him) rue Félix Pyat, I don't know how to spell it, I don't know the number, get moving.

The ticket was number 51708 (Group 2). It had been put on sale at the bar in rue Félix Pyat on the last Thursday in September along with twenty-three other tickets.

The proprietor of the bar thought that they were making a lot of fuss about nothing at all. In 1935 he had sold the ticket that won the big prize. He sold more than fifty tickets a year that won prizes of less than a million francs, and he didn't get any publicity from them. "The ticket that killed"; that might be fine for the headlines, but these gentlemen in Paris were old enough to understand that he could get along very nicely without that kind of publicity. Just look at it that way.

As for who had bought the ticket, he didn't have any idea. And for that matter, he didn't even know who had sold it. There were three of them in the bar: himself, his wife, and the *garçon*, Roger Tramoni, a good man, but he had asthma.

Wednesday night at six o'clock, when the man from the Lottery offices came to take back the unsold tickets, sixteen of the twenty-four had been sold. One of them was the winning one.

Georgette Thomas had come in on Tuesday night to meet Pierre Becchi. He was playing cards with friends. She had had an apéritif at the bar, talking to the owner's wife while she waited for the game to be over. She might have bought the ticket then, but if so, it was neither Monsieur Lambrot nor Madame Lambrot who had sold it to her, because Madame had gone back to the kitchen to start dinner, and Monsieur had not left the bar the whole evening.

They couldn't say definitely whether she had bought it without questioning Roger Tramoni, away on holiday in the Alpes-Maritimes where he always went for his asthma, and he wasn't the type who would remember anyway. They were going to find him and question him, but that would take time. In any case, these gentlemen in Paris didn't really think people went around committing murders for seven hundred thousand francs, did they? Granted, they might not need his advice, but just the same . . .

"People commit murder for much less than that," Tarquin said, "and she's the one who bought the ticket. She must be; it all fits together too well. Tuesday night, while she's waiting for her steward to pick up his chips, she has a glass of something at the bar and gossips a little with the owner's wife. Then, when the old woman goes out to the kitchen, she goes over to the tobacco counter, where this Tramoni is selling some stamps to somebody, and asks for a packet of cigarettes, and then she says, 'Let me look at your lottery tickets; maybe one of them has my lucky number.'"

Tarquin took a cigarette from the pocket of his shirt, looked for his matches, said give me a light, please; believe me, Grazzi, I can see it as clearly as if I were there, in full Technicolor.

"And Wednesday night she goes to break bread with her little steward, in the pizzeria. I can see it as if I were there. Soft lights, soft music, everything."

"There are no orchestras in pizzerias in the Saint-Mauront part of Marseille," Grazzi said. "I know; I've been there."

Tarquin got up, pointed his index finger at Grazzi's tie, walked around the desk and said, you see, that's just what I mean, that's why I'm always ahead of you, I like to get into things myself, I'm not satisfied with just seeing the sights. Maybe there wasn't an orchestra, but you can be sure there was a radio or a TV set.

"I don't understand."

"You never understand anything. Wednesday nights, do you ever listen to the radio? What do you think half of the people in this country are listening to on the radio on Wednesday nights? The draw on the National Lottery, that's what."

Grazzi said, all-right, all-right, then what?

"She didn't start dancing on the table," Tarquin said, "she didn't swallow her plate, she didn't even say anything. But her attitude had changed, maybe she didn't talk as much, and finally her boy friend noticed it and said, 'What's the matter? Are you tired?' and she answered, 'No, it's nothing . . . *And besides, I'm not sure.*' Because it's true that she wasn't sure. She had to wait until she got to her room, and he had gone out to the bathroom or something, before she could look at her ticket and make sure of the number. I tell you, I can see it as if I were there."

He stubbed out his cigarette, glanced at the clock, picked up the telephone almost before it began to ring, and said to Grazzi, "She was quite a girl, your little Georgette."

Grazzi chewed absent-mindedly at his thumbnail, thinking of all the nylon and lace marked with a little red G, of a dark-haired woman buying a newspaper as she left the hotel on Thursday morning, searching through it hurriedly to make certain she had won enough money to buy another Dauphine with initials on the doors. A thirty-year-old woman with a pleasant smile, who had kept it all to herself: her joy, her surprise, the excitement that made it impossible to sleep – but not the seven hundred thousand francs.

4:20 P.M.

Ticket number 51708 had been redeemed on Saturday 5 October, at about eleven-thirty, at the central office of the National Lottery, Croix-des-Petits-Champs, in Paris.

The tellers remembered the man who had brought it in. They had given him fourteen brand-new notes for five hundred new francs each, and he had seemed nervous as he put them in an old morocco leather wallet. They would surely be able to identify him. A good memory was indispensable in their profession.

Description: thirty-five to forty years old, long, thin face, prominent nose, light-brown hair combed high, to make him look taller probably, about five foot eight, very thin, pale complexion, grey overcoat, no hat.

Jouy telephoned from a bar near the Garaudy apartment. He had caught up with Evelyne Garaudy after lunch, and had been following her ever since. She had done some shopping at the Galeries Lafayette, in a little shop on Avenue de l'Opéra, and at the Louvre department store. She hadn't wasted any time, she knew what she wanted in every place she went: a jersey blouse, some shoes that Jouy said were very pretty, and two nylon petticoats, one pink, one white.

"If you could see all that," Grazzi said, "she must have seen you."

"She did, while she was in the Louvre. I talked to her. I calmed her down by telling her I was protecting her."

"Did you tell her about Rivolani and Darrès?"

"I had to."

"What did she say?"

"That it was terrible, that she was going home. Then she came home. I'm right opposite the house."

"Stay there."

Commissioner Tarquin's theory: Georgette Thomas wins seven hundred thousand francs – seven thousand new francs – learns about it from the radio in a Marseille pizzeria, but isn't certain she heard correctly. She verifies it the next day in the morning paper, but says nothing.

Examining Magistrate Frégard's question: Why would she say nothing about it?

Inspector Grazziano's reply: Initials on all her underclothes, on the linings of suits and dresses. Initials on the doors of the Dauphine. Egocentric, selfish nature. Besides, why say anything?

Tarquin's theory: someone, somehow, learns on Thursday or Friday that Georgette Thomas is in possession of a lottery ticket worth seven hundred thousand francs. He takes a berth on the Phocéen for Friday night, to follow her. For some reason she remains in the compartment after the other passengers have left, the someone either comes in or is already there, kills her, takes the lottery ticket, and goes to redeem it at rue Croix-des-Petits-Champs.

Frégard's question: Why kill her in the train, and run the risk of being seen or heard?

Grazziano's reply: It's the only possible time and place. The someone knows that she might go directly from the station and collect the money herself. In that case, the game is up.

Tarquin's theory: The someone who killed her collects the money, and keeps the new notes, if he isn't aware that we have a record of their numbers. If he is, he'll try to change them, fast.

Frégard's question: But why kill two other people from the same compartment?

Grazziano's reply: He made some kind of mistake, something that might get him caught, he thinks they witnessed it, so he eliminates them.

Frégard shook his head, seeming unconvinced: he knew there were criminals who would kill for less than nothing, for hardly enough to buy a packet of cigarettes. But the trick with the lift, in the case of Eliane Darrès, was too clever; it didn't fit in with that kind of mentality.

4:48

Report from the Préfecture de Police in Marseille: The owner of the Hôtel des Messageries, rue Félix Pyat, found twelve aspirin tablets in an ashtray on the bedside table in Georgette Thomas' room Friday night, after her departure.

Gabert telephoned shortly before five o'clock. He had checked every employment agency of any importance in Paris, with no results. He had had another idea about locating the girl from Avignon, and was coming back to the office.

Grazzi told him he would have news for him when he came in, then told him some of it over the phone. Jean-Loup whistled, and said, I hope I get back before you wind it up.

As he hung up the phone, Grazzi looked out the window behind Tarquin's desk and saw that the sun was gone. Night had fallen, and it was raining.

Interrogation of Georgette Thomas' ex-husband, Jacques Lange.

He was tall, older than Grazzi had thought he would be, a good-looking man, well dressed. He made no pretence of more sorrow than he felt, but it was obvious that he felt some. He sat very straight in his chair, smoking an English cigarette, not knowing any more than anyone else had known.

He said that Georgette was a child, that there was twenty years' difference in their ages, and he had never really been able to be angry with her. She had hurt him terribly, though, when he learned that she was deceiving him. He did not like the car salesman. He called him a worm. Grazzi, who had thought the same thing, just nodded. They were past all that now.

"Did she ever buy lottery tickets, while you were married?" he asked.

"Every now and then, just like everyone else."

"Do you know Bob Vatsky?"

"No. She mentioned him to me, though. I saw her occasionally, you know. I still work for Gerly, and she was with Barlin. Being in the same business, we couldn't help meeting from time to time."

"And Eric?"

"She mentioned him, too. I think that was more serious than Vatsky."

"Why?"

"If you could have heard her talk about him, you wouldn't ask why," Lange said. "He's young, he's almost a child, he has a child's mind and spirit. It's difficult to explain to someone who didn't know her. 'Little Eric' – she loved him the same way she loved herself; he's made the same way."

"I don't get it," Grazzi muttered.

"I know; I told you you wouldn't."

"Do you think he had something to do with Georgette's murder?"

"I didn't say that. But this murder doesn't make any sense. And anything that doesn't make sense fits in very well with both Georgette and her little Eric."

"You said you hadn't even met him."

"She described him to me very well, believe me. He's filled with ideas, about men and about animals, he dreams of some kind of laboratory in the jungle, he talks about things he knows nothing about: the world, the miseries of the world, and God knows what else . . . About six months ago she came to see me in my office, about this laboratory in South Africa or somewhere like that. She had no sense of reality at all. She wanted to get me to invest in the business. She said I owed it to her."

Grazzi was confused. "What business?" he asked.

"Don't ask me; I'm just telling you, that's the way they are. A laboratory in South Africa, you just take off and go to South Africa; that's the only kind of life, the real life. The next day they've forgotten all about it."

"It's too bad for him that she's dead," Grazzi said, half to himself. "She would have had enough to buy two tickets for the plane."

It was Lange's turn to be confused.

"He'll explain it to you," Grazzi said, and turned him over to Alloyau, who had come to relieve him for a few minutes.

He felt tired, and still worried, but he didn't know why.

Pardi found Cabourg at ten minutes to six. But by this time on that Monday evening, so many other things had happened that the second discovery, of the death of Progine's sales supervisor, came as almost no surprise.

In the inspectors' room, Mallet had pinned a pink file to the windowsill behind Grazzi's table. It was labelled "Rate per Corpse", and recorded graphically the murderer's return on his original investment in Georgette Thomas. From a high of 700,000 old francs, it had dropped to 233,333 with the deaths of Rivolani and Eliane Darrès. With the addition of Cabourg's name, it fell to a new low of 175,000 francs. The inspectors gathered around the chart were in agreement that, at those rates, it was a very risky business.

Grazzi had been studying the pink file uneasily when Pardi came in and sat down in the chair on the other side of the table.

"Cabourg?" Grazzi said, knowing what the answer would be.

Pardi nodded. "Listen carefully," he said, "it's worth it. I checked all the hospitals and the Commissariats first, but I found him in Boileau's office. He's the guy who got himself shot in the gents at the Central. No papers on the body. They didn't know who he was. Boileau's men found his fingerprints on file in the Commissariat at Gare de l'Est. He got an identity card there a few months ago. They came and told me while I was still on the telephone."

Boileau's office was on the same floor as Tarquin's, almost next door.

"When was he killed?" Grazzi asked.

"Saturday night, about eleven o'clock."

"The same kind of bullet?"

"Yes. In the back of the neck."

"What about their investigation?"

"Nothing. Not a clue. They thought it was probably a gambling thing – after all, the gents in a boxing stadium . . ."

Grazzi sighed wearily. Mallet had overheard them, and made the necessary change in his record.

Gabert telephoned a few minutes later.

"Where are you?" Grazzi said.

"In the Identification Bureau. I've got a new lead on the girl from Avignon."

"What is it?"

"Taxi drivers."

Grazzi ran a hand across his jaw, feeling the stubble of his beard. He always needed a shave by this time of day. He wished he could think of a way to put Pardi on the trail of the girl from Avignon without offending Jean-Loup. Pardi moved faster, and time was vital.

"Look," he said, "I need you here now."

"Oh, come on, chief," Gabert said, "I've almost got her; I promise you, I'll find her."

Grazzi nodded to the telephone, thinking, I'm going to regret it, they'll kill her first.

"I have to find her, do you understand?" he said, almost pleadingly. "It's vital that you find her, fast! This is a madman, and he isn't going to stop now."

"I'll find her," Jean-Loup said. "Don't worry about her, chief."

While they were talking, all the Commissariats in the Paris area were being asked to pass on to every policeman on duty a description of the girl. It wasn't very complete, but it was the best they could do: she was about twenty, blonde, pretty, and when last seen she had been wearing a blue coat.

It was five minutes past six.

Berth 223

Benjamine Bombat – known as Bambi – stood in front of the great doors to the main waiting rooms, huddled into her blue coat, listening to the sounds of the trains in Gare de Lyon. There was a boiled sweet with a strawberry centre in her mouth, the taste of a kiss on her lips, and an empty box of matches in her hand. She dropped the box in the gutter and said to herself, I've had enough, I've had enough, what have I done to the good Lord that this should happen to me?

It was a few minutes past six by the clocks in the station; she noticed it as she left. At least she wasn't crying any longer, that was something. She could always cry tomorrow morning, when she went into Monsieur Picard's office and he said, mademoiselle, you are very nice, you spell well and you are a good typist; I have no doubt of your sincerity or of the truth of what you say, but unhappily I must tell you that you're going to have to find a place somewhere else.

Monsieur Picard wouldn't put it that way, of course, but she would certainly be fired on her second day, like an idiot, like a goose, like the dingo girl she was.

It was Daniel who taught her the word "dingo". He said: a dingo character, the driver is dingo, I met a girl who is completely dingo. It meant: crazy, off your rocker, someone with fog in the head, fog in the eyes.

She wasn't crying any longer, but there was a kind of fog in her eyes, distorting the outlines of the square in front of the station and the buses going off in the direction of Place de la Bastille, misting over this city she had dreamed of so long, like a goose, like a dingo girl from the provinces.

Tomorrow she would be fired. They would probably even take the room away from her. It would be finished before it had begun. Three days ago, just three days ago, she had imagined that she would arrive in Paris with the appetite of a healthy young animal, the flashing white teeth of a healthy young animal, cleaned twice a day with Selgine – a really medical toothpaste – with her blue coat that was only a month old, with blonde hair and pretty legs and blue eyes that would break a man's heart, with good spelling and typing, a diploma from the École Pigier, three new dresses and three skirts in her suitcase, and fifty thousand francs in her handbag.

Instead of that, there had been this imbecile, this beautiful infant from the soap ads, this boy who didn't even have to shave, this spoiled child who considered himself God's gift to the world, who thought everyone else was dingo, who couldn't take a step without knocking you down and tearing your stockings, my baby, my darling, my love, Daniel.

She realized that she was in a bus, going towards the Bastille, and the conductor was asking for tickets. She gave him one, just enough to get to the Bastille; after that she would walk, no matter where, with the taste of a kiss on her lips and a strawberry sweet in her mouth, she would let the tears flow freely, no one would see them if she was walking.

He tore three pair of stockings, and I want to die, I swear I want to die if I'm never going to see him again.

As she got off the bus at the Bastille, with her arms hanging empty at her sides, because she had forgotten her bag when she dashed out of the office at four o'clock, she said to herself for the first time: I've been here before, and he was with me, it was wonderful and terrible; if Mother knew, she would faint, but I don't care, I don't care, what difference does it make, no one will see, I'll go ahead and cry.

The circle was enormous, black and shining in the rain, roped in far-off lights. She wept as she crossed it, thinking, I don't care, did I give him some money, at least, so he could eat on the train?

She had been here with him. There was almost no place she could go in this entire city without crossing one of the paths they had followed in those two days. When was it they had been here? Saturday. In a taxi.

I'm not going back to the room right away, she thought. I'll walk as far as the Palais-Royal, find some dark little café where I can get some eggs or something, read the newspaper while I eat, and then I'll walk back to rue du Bac. I'll go up to the room and straighten up and do the washing, just as if nothing had happened. Or maybe I'll go to some bar and behave like an idiot, talk to boys I don't know, dance, drink things that make you dizzy, that make you forget, but is there anything that could make you forget Daniel?

Three days ago, Friday night, she had kissed her mother and her little brother goodbye on the platform of the station at Avignon. As she got in the train she was smiling, a smile so happy her mother had said, "Aren't you even

135

a little bit sorry to leave us?" And she had answered, "We'll see each other in such a little while. At Christmas."

That was three months away, it was no time at all. And three days, what is three days?

He had been standing, straight and thin as a stick, halfway between the toilet and the connecting passage between the carriages, ready to flee into the next one the instant he saw a conductor, his raincoat over his arm, his tweed suit badly rumpled, with eyes like a whipped dog, so stupid it was unbelievable.

The train was pulling out. He leaned over to help her lift her suitcase, lost his balance, almost knocked her down, and tore the first pair of stockings.

She had said, please, I can do it myself, in her nastiest tone. She could feel the smarting in her ankle where he had kicked her. And the stocking was ruined; there was no point even in taking out her nail polish and trying to stop the run.

He hadn't apologized; he didn't know how. He stood there like a fool, saying, it's heavy, and watching her lift the hem of her dress to look at the stocking. Then he had said – and that was the last straw – it's gone; I have iron tips on the soles of my shoes, Mother made me get them, they tear everybody's stockings.

Holding up her dress at the side, with the train pulling out, wetting her finger tip with her tongue and applying it uselessly to the stocking, she had looked up, she had really seen him for the first time. A nice-looking face, fifteen or sixteen years old, the expression of a whipped dog, and she had said, it doesn't matter. She carried the suitcase to the compartment herself.

Standing in front of an open window in the corridor, there had been the woman, Georgette Thomas, and the man with the long nose, Cabourg. The woman, to let her pass, had just pulled herself in a little, turning to look at her with eyes she would never forget, she didn't quite know why (perhaps because the woman was dead), with eyes that seemed to know her already, eyes that said: there she is.

The compartment was terribly overheated, suffocating. There was a woman on the right, and a man on the left, in the lower berths. The man was snoring.

Bambi had stretched out awkwardly in her berth, thinking of her mother, of the three dresses she would have liked to take out of the suitcase and hang up properly, of the ruined stocking. She took off her stockings under the blanket, and finally managed to get out of her dress, thinking, after all, I can't sleep with it on, I wonder how people manage.

The blonde woman, Madame Darrès, who Daniel had told her later was an actress, was wearing pink pyjamas and a pink dressing gown. She was lying on top of the blanket because of the heat, reading a magazine and occasionally glancing up at Bambi.

"There's a light on the wall, just above your head," she had said.

Bambi had turned on the light, thanked her, and said, the trains are very comfortable now. But in fact it was the first time she had ever made an overnight trip. She had folded her dress against the partition, put her handbag and stockings by the pillow, and started to read her book, with a kirsch-centred sweet in her mouth. The conductors had come for the tickets a little later.

* * *

"Two eggs, scrambled, and a cup of coffee," the waiter said. "Are they done the way you wanted them?"

Bambi nodded absently. She was sitting alone at a table in a café near the Palais-Royal.

She read the article in *France-Soir* for the second time, but there was nothing in it. They had just rewritten the stories that had appeared that morning. The police would say nothing for the moment, but an arrest was imminent. She searched in vain for some mention of Inspector Grazziano, the one Daniel had said was the best of them all.

Her eyes must be red from crying, because the waiter had looked at her curiously when he brought the eggs, and turned around to glance at her over his shoulder as he left. She wished she had her compact, so she could powder her nose, but it was in the handbag she had left in the office, rue Réaumur. Fortunately her wallet was in the pocket of her coat, with the "Monday" handkerchief, wet with tears, and the sweets Daniel hadn't wanted.

The "Monday" handkerchief was one of her mother's ideas. In the train, when she saw Daniel again, she had had the "Friday" handkerchief, the red one with white polka dots.

When the conductors came in, she had sat up and reached down to the foot of the bed for the blue coat, clutching the blanket around her shoulders with her other hand. She found her ticket and gave it to the conductor standing nearest her. The other one was looking at the ticket of the woman with the dyed blonde hair, the actress. Then they had both woken up the man in the berth below Bambi; he seemed to go on snoring the whole time, but maybe that was just the way he breathed.

While they were busy and no one was looking at her, she slipped her arms into the blue coat and put on her shoes. As soon as they had left, she got down from the berth and went out into the corridor. Georgette Thomas and Cabourg were still talking, standing side by side in front of the open window. The dark-haired young woman was smoking, and the breeze from the window sent grey threads of smoke racing down the corridor. The silhouettes of trees against the sky flashed past, punctuated by the clicking of the wheels.

The toilet was occupied. She made her way through the connecting passage into the next carriage, but there was someone in that one, too, so she came back. The floor of the passage shifted beneath her feet, like the floor in the crazy house at the annual fair, and she had had to hold to the sides to keep her balance. Her fingers came away black.

She stood outside the door to the toilet, waiting. She could hear the conductors going into the other compartments, apologizing for waking people, asking for tickets. Finally she had seized the handle of the door and rattled it noisily, the way she used to do in school when one of the other girls was in the bathroom and wouldn't come out.

The door had opened just a crack, and the moment she saw his eyes, his frightened look, she had understood.

"What do you want?" he said. He had straightened up, like a little fighting cock, as soon as he saw that it was not the conductors at the door.

The idiot child who had torn her stocking. When she didn't answer, the fear came back to his eyes, and he whispered feverishly, "Don't stand there like that. Go away. I don't have a ticket."

"You don't have a ticket?" She had no idea why she

said that; she had known he didn't have a ticket when he opened the door.

"No. Don't talk so loud."

"I'm not talking loud."

"Yes you are."

It was just then that they had heard the conductors opening the door of the last compartment in the carriage, scarcely six feet from where they stood. *Pardon, messieurs – dames; vos tickets, s'il vous plaît.*

Daniel had grasped her arm and pulled her into the toilet, so hard and unexpectedly that she almost cried out. Then he reached behind her and latched the door. It was the first decisive move she had seen him make.

"No!" she said angrily. "Let me out of here!"

He put his hand across her mouth, just as Robert Taylor had done with Deborah Kerr in a movie she had seen in Avignon two months before. But Robert Taylor had a moustache, he was dark-haired and virile, and this was a blond child whose frightened eyes were pleading with her.

"Don't say anything, please. Just be quiet!"

They had stood there side by side, behind the locked door. She could see her face in the big mirror above the washbasin, and said to herself, "This could only happen to me; if Mother could see me, she would faint."

In the soft, unaccented speech that always betrayed a pupil of the Jesuits, he whispered in her ear that he had planned to hide on the outside steps, but there was someone standing in the corridor of the next car who would have seen him, and besides he was afraid he wouldn't be able to open the door to get in again, and he didn't know what to do with his suitcase.

The suitcase was underneath the washbasin – a big,

bulging thing of real pigskin. A spoiled child, a rich man's son, you could tell from looking at the suitcase, even if you didn't know already. His father was a lawyer and a town councillor in Nice; he had told her that the next day, and also that he had been in a Jesuit school in Toulouse, doing his second year again because he had failed in mathematics, that he was sick of the whole thing and had decided to go off and live his own life.

Someone knocked at the door and asked whether there was anyone inside. She pushed the boy away from her and put a finger on his lips, the way they used to do at school. He understood and backed into the corner; climbing up to stand on the toilet seat, looking like a fool and making too much noise. Before she opened the door, she unbuttoned her coat, so that they would think she really had been in the washroom: if Mother could see me, she would faint.

'Yes?"

"Oh, excuse me . . ."

She held the door partially open with her right hand, clutching the coat around her with her left. The younger of the two conductors retreated a step, and the other automatically lifted a hand to his cap. She must have been as white as a sheet. If she turned her head she would see herself in the mirror, with her bare legs showing beneath her coat, and she would be the one to faint.

"You have already taken my ticket . . ."

The older one said yes, yes, excuse me, mademoiselle, and they went on to the next carriage together. She closed the door, seeing herself in the mirror, her eyes as frightened as Daniel's, but just one knee showing beneath the coat. She wasn't white as a sheet; her face was violently flushed.

They stood there silently for a second or two, with him

141

crouched against the ceiling, his feet on the cover of the toilet seat, and her leaning against the door, holding her coat tight around her, knowing that something was happening to her, and knowing what it was, it's stupid, but that's the way it happens, something inside me, just looking at him. His face was flushed, too, with dark eyes that said thank you, so dumb it was unbelievable, my love, my Danny, my Daniel.

"You have a streak of black on your face."

Two minutes later, when they were certain the conductors had really gone, that was all he could think of to say.

Her dirty hands must have touched her face, somehow; or else he had done it himself when he put his hand across her mouth, the idiot. She wiped her cheek with her handkerchief, looking at herself in the mirror. He climbed down from the toilet seat, lost his balance and almost broke his neck, grasped at her for support; without saying excuse me because he didn't know how to say it. He smiled at her in the mirror. All he knew how to do was to smile, with that pretty, spoiled-child mouth of his.

"You do too," she said. "There . . ."

She handed him her handkerchief, pointing out traces of soot on his forehead and his beardless cheek. He wiped it off, standing very close to her. Then they had washed their hands with the SNCF soap, which had a strong, harsh smell, that of something made to be used by everybody.

He had looked at the red handkerchief with white polka dots, and laughed.

"When I was a child, I had some like that. One for each day of the week."

When he was a child! Sometimes when he spoke he had a slight Provençal accent, in spite of the remonstrances and punishments of the Jesuits – a refined, misshapen accent, like the rich boys in Avignon who didn't know how to say excuse me.

Suddenly then he had turned away from her, hiding his face, because he must have been thinking of his mother, of the handkerchiefs, of all sorts of things welling up in him and bursting like a wave.

A baby, a child. Daniel.

She was finishing the scrambled eggs, not wanting them but forcing herself to eat, when she remembered that the key to her room was in the handbag she had left in the office.

Daniel had left the door unlocked, he had told her that on the telephone. At four o'clock that afternoon.

It was Bambi's first day at the office. She knew, when they said, "It's for you," that there was no one else it could be.

"Bambi?" he had said.

"Yes."

"I had to leave the door unlocked; I didn't have a key."

"Where are you?"

"In Clichy."

There was a long, a very long silence, because she didn't know what to say, and neither did he, and it was embarrassing to be watched by all these new faces around her.

"Where is that – Clichy?"

"It's quite a way."

For them, that meant quite a way from Gare de Lyon. Every part of Paris was located by its distance from the spot where they had first looked on the chilly, grey city, two days before.

"Is it far from here?" she asked.

"I don't know."

Another silence, very long again, and then he had said, "I'm going away, Bambi."

She had not answered. What can you answer, when ten people are looking at you, and you are a goose?

"I think it's best to go back home," he went on hurriedly, urgently, "I'll explain everything to my father. He can go and talk to the police. You won't have any trouble, and neither will I. My father knows how to take care of things like this."

"How will you get there?"

"I'll take the train, just the way I came."

She had wanted to tell him, but she couldn't. If she told him about how she felt, and about all the other things, he wouldn't know what he should do. And there were all those people looking at her, petrifying her.

"Daniel . . ."

She had at least spoken his name, and perhaps your voice, and the way it pronounces a name, betrays everything that is breaking your heart, because suddenly all the people who had been watching her turned away, looking annoyed. Then she had heard him speaking very fast, saying wonderful things, terrible things, my little Bambi, Bambi, love, soon, always, night, someday, Paris, Nice, you, me, my little Bambi, listen Bambi, and he had hung up.

She had put down the telephone, walked back between the rows of tables and hammering typewriters without knocking anything over, without making a misstep, with a kind of smile that drew her lips back against her teeth. She had gone back to her work, she had even typed two or three pages, without lifting her head from the machine.

Then, suddenly, it had all been too much; she couldn't stand it any longer, nothing else mattered: she had stood up from her table, run to the rack where her coat was hanging, run through the entrance and down the street, and finally into the big hall of Gare de Lyon and out to the platforms. She saw then that it was only five o'clock, and the first train for Marseille-Nice-Ventimiglia left at 5:50, and she had waited . . .

She had left the toilet first, to make sure there was no one waiting outside the door. When he came out, they stood by the passage between the carriages and he told her that he had left home a week before and had hitchhiked to Cannes and then to Marseille, a dirty city where everyone asked questions. He had slept one night in a hotel, when he still had some money, two nights in a youth hostel, two in the waiting room of the station, and one in a bistro that stayed open all night.

"What are you going to do?" she asked him.

"I don't know."

He never knew anything. And because she was five or six years older, he had told her everything, trusting her; he had even called her madame. The thing that bothered him most was the suitcase. He was sorry he had brought it. Bambi was thinking, he has to get some sleep.

"There's an empty berth in my compartment," she said. "Wait out here a little while, and when there's no one in the corridor, you can come in. It's the upper berth on the left-hand side. Mine is underneath it."

He had looked at her with a kind of admiration, nodding eagerly at everything she said. It was then that he had called her madame.

The dark-haired woman and Cabourg were still standing by the window, just outside the compartment. Bambi had told him this, and then she had left him and gone to bed herself, warning him to give them time to get in bed after they went inside, and not to make any noise when he came in.

"What about the suitcase?" he said stupidly.

'What about it? Bring it with you, of course!"

It was the suitcase that caused all the trouble. That foolish pigskin suitcase. He had packed only two shirts and one change of clothes, but he had brought all kinds of incredibly silly things – books, a pair of boxing gloves, a sailing boat, some tins of food, a silver table service he was planning to sell, a bottle of Eau de Cologne, so he would smell nice, and no fewer than three hairbrushes, so he would look proper.

As if he didn't look wonderful anyway, Bambi thought, as she left the café and walked out into Place du Palais-Royal. They had been here, too, Sunday morning, yesterday, a thousand years ago.

They were following the little inspector in the duffel coat, taking taxis from one end of Paris to the other. Eleven hundred francs it had cost to go to rue La Fontaine, and then they had waited in a *bar-tabac* on the corner, seated at a table, watching the door across the street.

The inspector in the duffel coat had come in about half an hour later and gone directly to the telephone, without noticing them.

"He's making another mistake," Daniel had said. "The cops are all fada!"

"Fada" was another of his expressions, but it was one she knew, because they came from the same part of the country. It was part of her world as well as his; she liked that.

In the train, though, and for a day and a night after the train, she had been years older than he, she had still been madame.

There had been the argument in the corridor after Bambi went back to her berth. She had heard Georgette Thomas speaking very loud, sounding angry, and she had pulled back the curtain on the door so she could see what was happening.

Cabourg had his back to her, but even so, she could sense his shame and humiliation. The dark-haired woman was clutching at the jacket of her suit just below her shoulder, with her fingers outstretched and taut like the claws of a bird. She seemed to be protecting some object in the inside pocket of the jacket, something he had been trying to take away from her.

Bambi had guessed the sort of thing she was saying to Cabourg from the harshness of her voice, but she could not make out the words.

Georgette Thomas had come into the compartment a few minutes later. All of the lights were out, but Bambi had seen her stretch out on the berth across from hers as calmly as if the argument had never taken place. She was slender and quite tall, a long-legged silhouette, lying on her back, very straight. Bambi did not like her. She couldn't understand the look the woman had given her when she got onto the train – a strange, incomprehensible look, both frightened and frightening.

Some time later – it must have been twelve-thirty or one o'clock – Cabourg had come in. Bambi had seen him take off his coat and climb up to his berth, trying to be very quiet.

When they pulled into the station at Lyon, she could see flashes of light through the heavy curtain on the window, and hear voices and footsteps on the platform outside. That would be the men pushing carts, selling coffee in cardboard cups and sandwiches in waxed paper, just as they did in Avignon. After a few minutes the train left, and she fell asleep.

She was sleeping on her stomach, with her head cradled in her arm, when she heard the boy open the door of the compartment, very cautiously, and close it behind him. Then he had tripped over his own suitcase, lost his balance, and said God damn it, what have I done now?

That was exactly what she was asking herself: what had he done now? She had an insane desire to laugh, without knowing why: because she had to help him lift the suitcase up to the berth, because he clung to her for support, and she was half undressed, because he almost fell into her berth, saying God damn it again, and because he finally managed to climb into the other berth, still muttering to himself, undoubtedly paralysed with fright, a perfect little fool. For a long time after he got into the berth he didn't dare to move, but he kept whispering, at least I got here, I almost went into the wrong compartment.

Later on he had leaned over the side of his berth, just above her, so close that she could see his eyes. They had talked for a long time, a confused murmuring that must have been very annoying to the others, if they were awake. Some of the things he said brought the hysterical laughter bubbling back.

He was sixteen years old. He had been sixteen in July. They were born under the same sign of the zodiac. She had said that Cancer was a terrible sign; everyone born under it was crazy. He said, "Is that true, really?" in a tone of vast alarm, and then lifted his body back into his own berth for a minute, because the blood was rushing to his head, making him dizzy.

After that Bambi hadn't laughed again, because he talked about himself and he sounded very unhappy. One thing he did know was how to talk about himself. The train rolled on towards Dijon, towards Paris, carrying him away from his friends and his school, and away from his father. He had wanted a motor scooter when he was sixteen, and his father wouldn't give it to him, so they had quarrelled.

Bambi fell asleep while he was talking, lying on her back with the blanket pulled up to her chin, seeing a face above her, vanishing into darkness and sleep, a face she seemed to have known for a very long time, no, you must listen to me, you must go home, it's stupid to run off like that, clickety-clack, clickety-clack . . .

In the morning she had opened her eyes just in time to see him climb down, the tweed suit looking more rumpled than ever, the raincoat over his arm. As he passed her, he had leaned over her, whispered mademoiselle, and kissed her lightly on the cheek. She had thought, he can't have slept at all.

After that she must have fallen asleep again, because suddenly it was seven-thirty and the train was approaching Paris. The corridor was already crowded with passengers standing by the windows, smoking. She heard someone say that it was cold.

She had sat up, as best she could, to put on her dress. The dark-haired woman in the berth opposite smiled at her. The actress was already dressed, sitting on her berth with her suitcase beside her. It was impossible to get into

149

the dress and hold the blanket around her at the same time, and in the end she had thrown the blanket off, saying, it doesn't matter, the men are asleep. And all the time she was getting dressed, stretching out her legs to pull on the torn stockings, she had been conscious that Georgette Thomas was watching her. Once she had glanced up quickly, and found the other woman staring at her just as she had the night before, the same inscrutable look.

When she went to wash her face and brush her teeth, there were a great many people in the corridor. That was when she saw the man Daniel told her about later, but she hadn't paid any attention to him at the time. She remembered that he had been wearing a grey overcoat, a little too long for him, like her Uncle Charles', and carrying a blue-canvas beach bag with the coat of arms of Provence painted on it, the sort of thing tourists buy as a souvenir.

She hadn't been thinking about Daniel then. Or if she had, it had been a formless thing, of no importance. He had gone; he would get along somehow.

By the time she returned to the compartment, the train was pulling into the station. The man who had the berth beneath hers had put on a green leather jacket and was tying the laces on a pair of worn, very heavy shoes. Cabourg had left almost immediately after that, not saying goodbye, not looking at her or at anyone else; he must have been still ashamed of the argument last night. Then, just as the train stopped, the man in the leather jacket had left, carrying his old suitcase, saying goodbye, ladies, very politely.

Bambi had put away her wash things, nodding and smiling when the actress waved goodbye to her, a curious, affected little gesture. Eliane Darrès had held herself very straight as she went out, in spite of the obvious weight of her suitcase. A spicy scent of perfume lingered behind her.

The corridor was emptying rapidly. Georgette Thomas was standing in front of the drawn curtain at the window. "Mademoiselle . . ." she had said hesitantly.

They were alone in the compartment. Bambi was just putting on her blue coat. She felt fresh and well rested, because she had washed her face in cold water and combed her hair very carefully, in spite of the fact that someone was knocking irritably on the door of the toilet.

Georgette Thomas' face seemed very pale in its frame of very black hair, but her eyes were large and blue, like Bambi's. She was still looking at her in that strange fashion, turning away when Bambi looked at her.

She wanted to talk to her, Georgette Thomas said. She must talk to her. It was absolutely necessary. But Bambi had realized at once that she had nothing of any importance to tell her.

"You saw that man last night, didn't you?" she said. "It was frightening, wasn't it?" Her voice sounded as if she didn't really believe what she was saying, was just looking for something to say, expecting some kind of answer.

"Oh, you see people like that all the time," Bambi had said. "There's no reason to get upset about it."

She had picked up her suitcase and turned to leave. But Georgette Thomas almost ran across the compartment, and stood in front of the door, blocking her path, saying, it's terrible that there should be people like that, no, listen to me Mademoiselle Bombat, don't go yet.

Bambi had thought, how does she know my name? And at the same time she was thinking, that idiot boy will try to get out of the station through the restaurant or the offices; he doesn't have a ticket, I'll have to catch him.

She had finally shaken off the other woman, saying, please let me pass, someone is waiting for me. But the oddest thing had been that she was frightened, and she had sensed that Georgette Thomas was frightened too.

"I wonder what it was she wanted?" Bambi thought as she walked through Les Halles, feeling suddenly homesick from the familiar smells of fruits and vegetables in the stalls. By now he must be in Dijon, perhaps even further. Saturday morning in Dijon I was sleeping, nothing had happened yet, he was in the berth above me, perhaps he was still talking to me.

She was walking back towards rue Réaumur, almost without knowing it. She had left the office in the middle of the afternoon, on her first day at work, without saying anything to anyone. They would fire her tomorrow. There are nights when it seems that the Lord has turned his back on you, and left you with nothing.

Her application for the job, and the copy of her diploma, had been submitted by mail, and she had been hired by mail: eighty-eight thousand francs a month, less social security, a month's paid holiday, the cost of her ticket to Paris paid, and a top-floor room in rue du Bac, with running water and a gas ring.

Tomorrow, when he fired her, Monsieur Picard would undoubtedly take the room away too. The Lord would leave her nothing at all. Mother would have said, "Nothing but your eyes, to weep."

She could, however, go back to the office tonight. Monsieur Picard might be working late, and she could see him and explain. He seemed to be a very nice man, and he might have a daughter just about her age. She would say, if your daughter had seen Daniel, standing by the exit from the platform in Gare de Lyon, the way I saw him that morning, she would have felt sorry for him too. But then she would have to explain about the room, the first night and the second – things that couldn't be explained.

It was useless to think like this. Monsieur Picard wouldn't be in the office in the first place. It was night, and it was cold; he would have gone home long ago. All she could do at rue Réaumur would be to rouse the concierge and pick up her handbag.

At eight o'clock on that Saturday morning he had been standing at a safe distance from the platform exit, where the station attendants collected the tickets. His hands were in the pockets of the raincoat, and he had a woman's scarf around his neck. Passengers brushed against him constantly as they passed, but he refused to move out of their path, a real little fool.

Bambi had put her suitcase down and said, what on earth are you doing, just standing there; what are you going to do?

He had sighed. "At last! What have you been doing all this time?"

"What do you mean, what have I been doing!"

"You didn't bring my suitcase?"

"Your suitcase?"

"But you agreed __."

"What are you talking about? What did I agree to?"

He shook his head, not seeming to understand, and she shook hers, because she didn't understand. They sat down on a bench, with Bambi's suitcase between them. He kept re-arranging the scarf, tucking the corners into the collar of his raincoat. It had a painting of the Bay of Nice painted on it.

"That's a woman's scarf," she said.

"It's one of Mother's. I don't know why I took it when I left. When I was a child, I used to love to wear Mother's things. Now, I don't know, it seems silly . . ."

The idea for getting out of the station had been his. He said he had told her about it during the night, and explained what she should do. She hadn't heard him, though; it must have been after she fell asleep.

"You were supposed to take my suitcase. You could get off the platform with your ticket, leave the suitcases in the hall, and then get two platform tickets, as if you were meeting someone, and come back. Then we could both get out, with the platform tickets."

"I didn't understand that. I didn't hear you. You certainly have some marvellous ideas!"

He had looked at her with a combination of disappointment and mistrust. You simply couldn't believe anything adults said. They didn't listen to you.

She had put a hand on his arm, trying to reassure him, wishing she were sure of herself. She said to herself, now I am really being stupid, what I should do is tell him to go and give himself up right away, and go home. At the worst, they'd send him to bed without his dessert.

"Go and get your suitcase," she said. "Where did you leave it?"

"In the compartment. On the luggage rack."

"Go and get it, and come back here."

"We'll do what I said?"

"Yes; we'll do what you said."

"And you won't leave without me?"

She looked straight at him, feeling oddly happy, almost

triumphant, the way she sometimes had at school, but stronger. This was better than fooling a teacher.

"What do you take me for?" she demanded.

He had nodded, confident and happy again, and run off towards platform M to get the suitcase.

She had waited for ten minutes, sitting on the bench, thinking, I know myself, I know myself only too well, I'll never have the courage to leave him without anyone to look after him, I'm going to get myself into all kinds of trouble, I'm mad.

When he came back with the suitcase, he was no longer running; and his face looked very odd: serious, thoughtful, almost unrecognizable.

"What's the matter?" she had said.

"What do you mean? Nothing's the matter."

She had gone out alone, carrying the two suitcases and her handbag. It was very heavy. In the hall she had to search through her wallet and all of her pockets to find two fifty-franc pieces, and then she bought two platform tickets from an automatic vending machine. She left the suitcases hidden behind the machine and went back.

He was waiting for her by the bench on the other side of the gate, with that same odd expression on his face, and it was then that she had remarked, "What have you done with your scarf?"

"I must have left it in the train," he said, fingering the collar of his raincoat and glancing back towards the track where the train still stood. "Come on, it doesn't make any difference."

Bambi had handed the platform tickets to the ticket collector at the gate, and they had gone out without incident. A moment later they were standing on the pavement outside the station, with their suitcases in their hands, on a cool, sunny morning, in the midst of crowds of people and swarms of buses and taxicabs.

"Well," Daniel said, "goodbye."

He didn't know how to say thank you, either.

"What are you going to do?" Bambi asked.

"Don't worry about me. I'll be all-right."

"No," she said stubbornly, "I am worried about you."

They had started to walk automatically, and they had to go some distance before Bambi saw an empty taxi and signalled for it. She got in, and he stood on the pavement, looking unhappy.

"Well," she had said, "are you coming or not?"

"Where?"

She hadn't known what to answer. He had trouble getting the pigskin suitcase into the taxi. He always had trouble with everything. They had been jammed against each other in the seat, with Bambi's dress up above her knees, but there wasn't room enough for her to pull it down, in a car that stopped and started with a series of violent jerks, driving through unknown streets, past unknown people.

She had given the driver the address that had caused her heart to beat faster every time she thought of it for the past two weeks. What would it be like, rue du Bac? When they crossed the river (Seine; source in the Plateau de Langres; empties into the Channel at Le Havre, 776 kilometres long), she had looked over at Daniel, who was occupied with his own thoughts. Because she needed to reassure herself, as well as him, she had said that everything would work out all-right. He had put his hand on hers without saying anything, a warm hand with long fingers tanned by the sun.

In rue du Bac there had been all sorts of trouble about finding the key to her room. There was no concierge in the building, so they had inquired in a *bar-tabac* next door, and then from the tenants on the other floors. Bambi had discovered that people in Paris were not very friendly.

At last it turned out that a girl named Sandrine already had the key, and was waiting for her in the room. She worked in the office on rue Réaumur, too; she had come to Paris from Nantes a year before. She had a room just like this one, in rue de Sèvres, and since it was near by, Monsieur Picard had asked her to come and meet Bambi and explain things to her. She said that it was disgusting to work in an estate agent's office and have to live in rooms like these. She looked at Daniel, wondering who he was and waiting to be introduced. But Bambi, standing on a stool with her hands in the pockets of her blue coat, staring out of her own window at the roofs of Paris, had forgotten about Daniel.

"I don't have the keys," the concierge at rue Réaumur said. "Even if there was a fire up there, I couldn't do anything about it."

"I just want to get my handbag," Bambi explained.

"It doesn't matter what you want – the typewriters, or the money in the safe – it wouldn't change anything. I don't have the keys."

Bambi turned on her heel and walked towards the staircase.

"Where are you going?"

"Up to the office. There may be someone there."

"There isn't anyone. They've all gone. Do you know what time it is?"

It was nine o'clock. She walked up all the same, rang the bell at the door on the second floor, and walked down again. The concierge was still standing in front of his door. He didn't say anything. He watched her go out into the night, thinking what a crazy generation, if she were mine I'd give her a good smack, or something of the sort.

The room was about twelve foot by nine, with a slanting mansard roof, and walls painted white. A screen in one corner concealed a gas ring, a cupboard, a basin, and – an unexpected luxury – a shower with a lemon-yellow plastic curtain.

"I can fix it up nicely," Bambi said.

Sandrine had stayed with them quite a while. "Your dress is nice," she said. "Your hair looks nice; how do you do it? Your shoes are nice. The shower is nice, don't you think?"

She thought everything was nice. While Bambi unpacked and tried to decide where to put things, she told them about the office, a long monologue which only she paid any attention to. The office was nice.

Suddenly, then, it was almost noon, Sandrine had left, saying something about seeing them that evening, and Daniel had gone to sleep on the bed.

The room looked different already, transformed by the photographs on the night table, books on a shelf, and the big soft bear on the bed. Daniel had caught it under his arm in his sleep, and it was rubbing against his cheek.

Bambi took a shower and put on the red towelling dressing gown she had bought with her mother at the same time as the big bath towels.

She found Daniel sitting on the bed when she got out of the shower, carefully looking away from her. The noise of the water must have woken him.

"You're going to have a shower too," she announced. "You must be filthy, sleeping in waiting rooms and bars. I don't want any fleas in here; and besides, it will give me time to get dressed."

She glanced over at the shower as she dressed, glimpsing a vague silhouette through the yellow curtain. He must be as skinny as a rail, she thought, and wondered what she was going to do with him.

"How can I get out of here?" he asked plaintively.

She handed him the towelling dressing gown, and he came out with his hair dripping water, the sleeves of the dressing gown only half covering his long arms and the seams at the shoulders about to split. She was still in her slip, looking for a pair of stockings to replace the ones he had torn.

That was the moment he chose to look at her unhappily and say, "There was a dead woman in the compartment."

If we had gone to the police right away, Bambi thought, nothing would have happened. I wouldn't be fired tomorrow, and I could write to Mother and tell her everything was all-right.

She came to Place du Châtelet, where there were a lot of neon lights, a statue, and a bridge across the river, straight ahead. She started across it, thinking, by this time he must have passed Dijon, but he's perfectly capable of changing his mind, getting off, and taking another train back here. I can see him now, knocking on my door at two o'clock in the morning.

With him, things that never happen happened all the time.

That Saturday they had left the room at one o'clock in

the afternoon, after sitting on the bed side by side, talking in whispers, like conspirators. Neither of them could possibly have discussed such an event in a normal tone of voice.

"When I left you by the bench," Daniel had said, "I went straight back to the train. I couldn't remember which carriage we'd been in, but finally I found it. As soon as I was in the corridor, I heard voices. They were coming from our compartment, so I went into the compartment next to it, to wait. They were men's voices, two of them. One of them did most of the talking; he sounded almost as if he were giving orders. The other one sounded as if he were sick; he had a nasty cough. It wasn't until later, when I was thinking about it in the taxi, that the coughing reminded me of something else. At the time, I didn't pay much attention. I didn't have any reason, then, to try to hear what they were saying. I was just waiting for them to leave. I was afraid they might be conductors, and would ask for my ticket. But that wasn't all I was afraid of; there was something about the way they were talking that frightened me, even without being able to understand what they said. They didn't stay very long, though – just about two minutes, maybe a little longer. I heard the door being opened and closed again, and then they were gone. I didn't see them because they didn't pass the compartment I was in; they went in the other direction, towards the exits from the station. I gave them time to get out of the carriage and then I went into the compartment to get my suitcase. That dark-haired woman who was talking in the corridor last night was lying across the bottom berth on the right. I've never seen a dead person before, but believe me, she was dead. You could tell just by the way she was lying there. I didn't know what to do, so I just grabbed my suitcase and left, and closed the door behind me. I don't think anyone saw me; there wasn't anyone else on the train."

He repeated the same phrases over and over; almost the exact same words. At first Bambi had thought the whole story was nonsense, but then she realized that he was genuinely worried, and tried to discuss it with him seriously, to work out what could have happened.

"You said that the voice of the man who seemed to be sick reminded you of something. What was it?"

"When we left Marseille last night, I was sitting on that little bench against the wall, just outside the entrance to the toilet. There was a man standing at the end of the corridor in the carriage behind ours; I could see him through the passage between the cars. He never stopped coughing, and every now and then he looked in my direction, as if he were watching for something. He was wearing a grey overcoat and carrying a blue beach bag with a coat of arms on it – it was the coat of arms of Provence; I had the same thing once on the pocket of a blazer. This morning he was standing in the corridor in our carriage. I could recognize him if I saw him again; he was pale and very thin; he looked sick."

Bambi was beginning to think the whole thing was nonsense again. She was hungry, and she was getting a headache.

"Get dressed," she said abruptly. "You look silly in that dressing gown. We'll get something to eat, and maybe then we can think of what we should do."

Daniel began to dress, turning his back to Bambi. She could not help noticing that there were holes in his socks, his pants were more nearly grey than white, and there were black streaks on the collar of his shirt.

She was horrified. "Don't you have any clean clothes with you?" she demanded.

"I haven't had time to wash anything in the past week," he said, "and I wouldn't know how to anyway. Can't you turn around?"

Without asking his permission, she opened his suitcase and began looking through its contents. When she found the big box containing the silver service, she thought, it isn't possible, I'll have to try and talk some sense into him, make him write to his parents, go home.

"You can at least change your shirt," she said. "There's another one here."

"It has grease all over it."

He had fallen into the grease pit in a garage. The truck that took him to Marseille had stopped, and he had wanted to look at the engine from beneath.

"I missed one of the steps," he said.

Bambi shook her head. Without knowing quite why, she put on the same dress she had worn on the train; she didn't have the courage to wear one of the new ones.

When they went out, however, she wished she had worn something warmer; it was colder in Paris than it was in Avignon. They walked for a long while, and by the time they went into a restaurant it was almost two o'clock. The place was empty, and they began to discuss the whole thing again, still keeping their voices to a whisper, because the two waitresses were watching them. Bambi wanted to go to the police and tell them everything they knew, right away. But even as she told him this, she knew she didn't really want to do it, because of her mother, and her job, and smuggling Daniel into the empty berth. He didn't want to either, because of his father, and in any case it was none of their affair. The police could handle it themselves.

The restaurant was very pleasant, with little curtains at the windows and gaily coloured Breton plates on the tables. Daniel ordered snails, after asking Bambi if that would be too expensive, and he drank a half bottle of rosé, which came from Bandol, very near his home in Nice. He wasn't accustomed to drinking, and since he did not eat much – he was too busy talking – he was a little intoxicated by the time they finished their meal.

He smoked Bambi's cigarettes, with his eyes sparkling and pink spots on his cheeks. She thought he looked wonderful like that, and wondered again what she was going to do with him.

They walked again, after lunch, back towards rue du Bac. She bought some Gitanes in a *tabac* (she didn't like them herself, but he said he preferred them to American cigarettes), and he took one from the packet, and then suddenly he had said, I'm going to see about it anyway; I have an idea. He had left her standing on the pavement in Boulevard Saint-Germain, and dashed across the street, narrowly escaping death in the mass of cars. When he reached the other side, he turned around for a second and shouted something about coming back that evening, to pick up his suitcase. She just stood there watching him, thinking, he's going to do something even more stupid, but now that I've begun I'll have to go on with it; I can't just let him go. And then he was gone.

Bambi stopped near the statue of Henri IV at the tip of the Ile de la Cité and took another sweet from the pocket of her coat. Two lovers were standing by the gate to the little garden beside the river with their arms wrapped tightly around each other. The sweet had an orange filling this time.

If she followed the bank along the Seine opposite the Tuileries Gardens, she would come to rue du Bac. She would get undressed in the darkness, so she wouldn't see all the things that could remind her of last night; she would lie face-down on the pillow and talk to herself until she went to sleep.

She thought of Daniel, standing at the door of the railway carriage three or four hours earlier. Why was it that he no longer looked like the foolish boy she had first seen on another train, three nights ago? Why do things change from one night to the next, so suddenly that you no longer recognize yourself?

She hadn't seen him until just about five minutes before the train left, running down the platform with his suitcase in one hand and the raincoat in the other, his eyes bigger and darker than ever, his face lined with fatigue, seeming much older.

In the time she had been waiting for him, she had bought him a ticket on the train, a newspaper, and a little bag of sweets and asked if there was a dining car. And when he arrived at last, and was standing in front of her, she did not try to make him stay.

"What did you do?" he asked. "Did you leave the office?"

"Yes."

"You're mad."

"What do you mean by that?"

"Just that. You're mad."

"You're driving me mad!"

She regretted having said that, almost at once. It was

cowardly of her; it would hurt him. He hadn't wanted the sweets.

"I think I understand now," he said.

"Understand what?"

"All of this business. They may be going to kill someone else. At least, I think they may."

"Who are they going to kill?" she said weakly. She really didn't care – not now.

"I don't know. That's why I have to go home, to talk to my father. He knows about things like that. The prefect of police comes to dinner all the time. They won't give us any trouble."

He had kissed her then, very gently.

She must have looked like a fool, standing there holding the sweets he didn't want, thinking that she would have welcomed trouble with open arms if only he would stay. She had prepared the words she would speak to him, imagining the scene a hundred times while she waited. And in the end, they had said nothing. He was tired, worried about her and about himself; he was thinking of nothing but the murder. He was a boy. They look at you and think about something else, and then, after they are in the train, they suddenly wonder if they kissed you goodbye and they are miserable.

At the last moment, standing on the steps, when he realized that the train was moving, he had looked at her and he had really seen her, running along beside him in her blue coat, with the bag of sweets in one hand and 2,000-franc notes in the other, holding them out to him.

And all he could find to say had been, "Damn it, don't leave me like this."

"I'm not the one who's leaving you!" she had shouted. She was running beside the train now. He had taken the money and was waving it at her, like a handkerchief.

She felt as if she were going mad; really mad this time, running along the platform, waiting for him to say something, anything at all that would help her to go on living.

And all he said was, "I'll send it back to you!"

The train was going faster than she could run, and he was leaning out of the door; he was so clumsy he would probably fall out. It was all too unjust, too unfair, and she had cried out, "Daniel!"

"There's a note for you in the room! It's true; there is!"

He had cried out, too. And then there was nothing: 2,000-franc notes waving in the distance like a handkerchief, and the crowd of people around her as she turned back towards the exit. When she got outside, she saw that the rain had stopped, and stood for a moment against the door of the station, huddled in her blue coat. There was a sweet with a strawberry filling in her mouth, and the taste of a kiss on her lips. She was holding an empty box of matches in her hand – it must have been in her pocket – and she dropped it in the gutter.

Saturday night, Sandrine had come to her room about six o'clock. They had waited for Daniel together, talking about the office, about Avignon, about Nantes. Sandrine was blonde, too, but thinner than Bambi. She said that Bambi looked like Dany Robin, but younger. She thought Bambi was very nice.

Finally, tired of waiting, they had left a note on the door and walked the few blocks to Sandrine's room in rue de Sèvres.

It was considerably larger than Bambi's. There was a little entrance hall, and a real kitchen. Sandrine had already laid the table, with three places because she had expected Daniel to come too. She had made *gratin dauphinois* and a filet of beef with peas.

"Does he like that?" she asked.

"I don't know," Bambi said. "He's a sort of a cousin; I don't know him much better than you do."

Daniel had arrived at ten o'clock, after they had finished dinner. He seemed to be living in some other world: when he came in, he kissed them both on the cheek, like well-brought-up children at a birthday party.

He ate almost nothing, and didn't say a word. After they left, he confessed to Bambi that he had had a steak in a restaurant near Gare de l'Est.

"Did you have some money?" she asked.

"I took a thousand francs from your bag this morning while you were in the shower."

All the way to rue du Bac, she had been too hurt and angry to speak to him. In front of the door to her building, he had looked down at the pavement, shuffling his feet awkwardly, and murmured, very rapidly, that she must not be angry with him, he really hadn't known what to do. He kept repeating, it's terrible, terrible.

"What's terrible? To have to write to your mother and father, and ask them to forgive you? You don't have any conscience, that's the thing that's terrible." The phrase pleased her. It made her feel protective, older and stronger than he. She was astounded at how much older and stronger she felt.

It was eleven o'clock. The building was completely silent, except for a hot-water pipe somewhere, knocking. Bambi took the mattress off the bed and set it on the floor, folding one of the sheets over it and the other one over the box spring. She didn't look at him, and he didn't look at her. Because he was an only child, and had been educated by the Jesuits, he got into the shower and undressed behind the curtain.

When he came out, he was wearing a pair of striped pyjamas with the initials D.C. embroidered above the pocket – his last name was Cravero; she knew that much by now. He looked at Bambi like a repentant child. She had put on a white nightdress and she realized that without her high heels she was shorter than he was.

He stretched out on the mattress on the other side of the room with one arm beneath his head, sighing noisily. She turned out the light and went to bed herself, feeling vaguely uncomfortable, but more cross than uncomfortable, really.

It was then he had told her that it was what had happened on the train that was terrible, not what had happened to him. If she hadn't been angry with him because of the thousand francs, which he would give back to her in any event, he would have shown her the newspaper.

She turned on the light again, and read the paper.

"They're sure to find you," he said. "They have your name."

"There are a lot of people named Bombat."

"It's not only that; it's much worse than that."

He told her that the idea he had had, when he left her after lunch, was that it had been a policeman arresting the murderer that he had heard in the compartment, but he knew now that he was wrong.

"Maybe it was just the wine," he said, "but I kept thinking about the sick man, and I was sure that was what had happened. A policeman came in, I don't know why or how, but he found him there and arrested him. Now, I don't understand at all."

"It's all stupid," she said irritably.

But when Daniel was there, the more stupid it was, the more likely it was to be true.

We talked for an hour or more, Bambi thought, as she walked up rue du Bac. He ate the steak while he was waiting for Cabourg, he took a thousand francs from my bag, he had thought about Progine, about telephoning Progine and following Cabourg, because he had an argument with the woman. He fell asleep while he was still talking. On my mattress, on the floor. The next morning he helped me put the bed together again. That was yesterday, Sunday.

"Where are you going today?" he said. He thought she was going out, because she had put on the black dress. It fitted her perfectly, and she looked good in black.

"Nowhere," she said firmly. "I'm going to clean the room, and wash your things. And you're going to write to your parents."

She had been able to see it very clearly, just the two of them, Daniel and Bambi, quietly together, forgetting all about the murder, never mentioning it again; and him, sitting at the table, writing his letter, while she sewed the curtain material she had bought at the Bon Marché on Saturday afternoon. Later they would say goodbye very fondly, and every year he would send her a card at Christmas, reminding her of the passage of time, and of how long ago that Sunday had been.

Nothing like that had happened. She had not sewn the

curtains. He had not written his letter. He had dragged her along with him, from one taxi to another, from Quai des Orfèvres to the Trocadéro, from Clichy to the race-course at Vincennes, determined to follow through on his foolish ideas, Daniel Cravero, boy detective, in a rumpled tweed suit.

She had scarcely had time to wash his shirts and underwear before they started out. When they came back that night, everything was dry, hanging on a line across the room, one of his vests just next to a lace slip of hers. Even if they don't take the room away, Bambi thought, I'll never be able to stay here now.

About noon, when they were following the dark-haired boy (Daniel hadn't seemed much younger than either the dark-haired boy or the blond inspector) there was one moment when they were squeezed together in a corner of the staircase in the apartment house on rue Duperré, not daring to move or even to breathe, for fear of being caught. Daniel's mouth had been so close to hers that Bambi could think of nothing else, in spite of what was happening. She had only kissed two boys in her entire life: one of her cousins, when she was thirteen, to see what it was like, and a boy from her philosophy class later, at a party, because she had drunk three glasses of champagne and he was very stubborn. But Daniel hadn't been thinking about her at all, even though his arm was behind her back and his body was pressed tight against hers. His mind was on other things. That was when he had torn the second pair of stockings.

By the time they finally stopped and had dinner, in a noisy restaurant on the *quais*, she was exhausted; it seemed to her that they had been in every corner of Paris, following his foolish ideas. She talked to him about Avignon, because she didn't want to hear another word about the murder. Walking back to the room, she had taken his hand in hers and held it all the way to rue du Bac.

"I'm sorry I tore your stockings," he said when they were back in the room. It was the first time he had said he was sorry for anything.

And he hadn't turned away while she took them off. They had just looked at each other silently, for a long time, while she sat on the bed with the stockings in her hand, in her bare feet and her black dress, and he stood there, still wearing his raincoat. Then she had said something stupid, that she was sorry – what was she sorry for? – and then, why are you looking at me like that?

He hadn't answered her. Instead he said would it be all-right if he stayed here tonight, anyway? She had wanted to ask what he meant by anyway? But she hadn't been able to.

He sat down beside her on the bed, still in his raincoat, and then she had made the little bargain with herself: she had told herself, if I'm going to prison tomorrow, and he goes to prison too, Mother will faint anyway. I'm going to kiss him, I can't help it.

She had leaned towards him, in her bare feet and her black dress, and kissed him, very gently, thinking, I can't help it, I can't help it.

He had not done any of the things she expected. He just lowered his head, swiftly, put his arms around Bambi's legs, and stayed there, motionless, silent, with his face buried in her lap, like a little boy.

Tonight, just as she had done on Saturday night and Sunday night, Bambi guided herself by the sign above the *bar-tabac* next door to her building on rue du Bac. It was just another red light in a swarm of red lights from the cars and the traffic lights, but she knew it, and trusted it.

The light in the hall stayed lit for just one minute, and then went out automatically, so she had to stop on the second floor and push the button again. She could hear the knocking of the faulty hot-water pipe; it was the only sound in the building. She went up the steps very slowly, thinking: motionless, silent, a little boy. Later, much later, his arms had moved up around her body, the long, thin hands she had watched in the restaurant an hour before, as if she had known already.

He tore the third pair of stockings the next morning – this morning! – when he pulled her back on the bed, after she was half dressed. He had said, damn it, you can't leave now, and she pretended to be angry with him, so he would be gentle again, as he had been during the night, and because the morning was different from the night, and she had difficulty recognizing him and recognizing herself. But it was true, there was the same gentleness on his lips; the night had not been a dream.

Fourth floor, one more to go. The light went out again – it must be broken; it couldn't have been a minute. She reached out, searching for the button, groping in the darkness. I searched for his lips in the darkness, I stayed awake in his arms all night long, my Daniel, my Danny, my love, I can't help it about Mother, I can't help it about the job, the light is on again.

What did he mean at the station, when he said he thought he understood now? What was it that he didn't tell me? At noon she had taken a taxi from the office – she shouldn't have done it, she had spent much too much money, but she couldn't bear to waste a minute, she was a trifle drunk from lack of sleep and the noise of the typewriters. Her lips were still bruised from his kisses, and all morning she had thought that everyone in the office must know what had happened. She had met him in the restaurant where they had lunch on the first day, the one with the Breton plates. There were a lot of people today – it was Monday, not Saturday – and they had looked at each other across the table, unable to speak a word. She knew he had been following his idea all over Paris again, but he said nothing about it.

Bambi arrived at the fifth-floor landing, thinking, I'll go to bed in the dark, I'll read the note he left tomorrow morning, I don't want to read it now, and then, yes, I do want to read it. It was terrible, at noon, we didn't know what to say to each other. I wanted to hurry, so we could come back here for a minute, and he understood, I whispered all sorts of foolish things in his ear. *My God, it's true, he came back, it's Daniel, he's there.*

She could see a ray of light under her door. She thought for a minute she was mistaken, but she wasn't; it was her door. *He changed his mind again; he's there!*

She crossed the landing in the darkness, because the light had gone out again, hands held out in front of her, everything in darkness except the streak of light on the floor and the keyhole, outlined as sharply as an eye, thinking it isn't possible, he couldn't have got off and taken another train and been back already, it does look like an eye, waiting for me. She almost ran into the door, and into the room.

The shot from the revolver had left a bitter odour. Sandrine was lying on the floor against the bed with her legs folded weirdly beneath her, as if her body were stuffed with straw. She had knocked over a stool as she fell, and her hand still grasped desperately at the red fabric of the bed cover, red as the horror that had been her face.

On the night table next to the note Daniel had left – a sheet of paper folded into a square – the shiny black leather of Bambi's handbag reflected the light from the ceiling, round, yellow, blinding.

An instant later – or two hours, three hours later, she didn't know – there was a room in some unknown hotel in a street near the Invalides, and Bambi was standing with her forehead pressed against the pane of the window, in her blue coat, alone, the rain streaming down the window, beating against her face; but not touching it.

She still had Daniel's note in her right hand, *I love you*, crumpled, illegible, torn, nothing else but that, a little ball of paper she pressed against her mouth, clenched in her teeth.

It was the only support she had left, this *I love you* clenched in her teeth, nothing else, don't think of Sandrine, opening the unlocked door of my room to bring me the bag, don't think of the horror of Sandrine's face, don't think: it was my face, I was the one who should have been lying there, grasping at the bed cover. Tomorrow I will go to the police. I love you, I'll wait until you're safely in Nice, until they can't hurt you, I won't think of anything else, just this *I love you*, nothing else.

Berth 225

Evelyne Berthe Jacqueline Garaudy, maiden name, Laverte; twenty-seven years old, attractive, well dressed, long brown hair, five foot four; distinguishing marks or characteristics: furtive look, lying tongue, stubborn, irritating personality. Her great blue eyes opened wide with horror as she contemplated the pink file Mallet had torn from its place on the windowsill and waved in front of her across the width of Grazzi's table. With the murder of the girl from Avignon, the "rate per corpse" had dropped another thirty-five thousand francs.

"Five!" Mallet said. "Don't you think that's enough?"

"You're mad! That's a horrible thing to do!"

She put her pretty hands to her pretty face and began to cry again.

"Why don't you stop lying to us?"

"I'm not lying!"

"Do you really want to be number six on this thing?"

"What do you want me to say? I don't know anything."

Mallet sighed. "There were six people in that compartment And you're the only one of them who is still alive. The others didn't know anything either. Very well – someone put a bullet in their heads because they didn't know anything. So tell me what it is that you don't know!"

She shook her head stubbornly. Mallet tore the pink file into little pieces, and dropped them in the wastebasket beside his chair.

"Keep on with it," Grazzi said, "and good luck."

He left the office with a sick, heavy feeling in his stomach. Weariness, dejection, nausea.

"How is it going?" Tarquin asked.

"She's as stubborn as a mule," Grazzi said, "but I think she'll talk in an hour or so, perhaps before noon."

He sat down on the arm of a chair beside Tarquin's desk, his legs crossed, his notebook in his hand.

The morning papers had all had the story of the murders of Cabourg, Rivolani, and Eliane Darrès. In the 38 bus on his way to the Quai, Grazzi noticed that all of the passengers turned and looked out of the window as they passed the Progine office where Cabourg had worked.

"Reports are coming in from everywhere," he said. "Two days ago we could have used them all, had something to go on. But now . . ."

'What kind of reports?" Tarquin asked.

"Progine, first. Saturday afternoon someone telephoned and asked for Cabourg's home address. A man's voice. He said he was a customer, making up his Christmas lists. It may be true. It may also be the way our man found the poor guy."

Grazzi turned a page in the notebook. "Rivolani, next. He owed money."

"So do I," Tarquin said.

"Darrès. When they went over her apartment they found some bank statements, but no chequebook."

"What of it? She probably finished one and hadn't had time to get another. What are you getting at?"

"The thing that bothers me is that I'm pretty sure I saw a chequebook."

"Where?"

"In her apartment when I brought her handbag in from the lift. It was open. I left it on a chest in the bedroom."

"It would be the first time they ever lost anything in the Identification Bureau. Brains, they don't have, but they don't lose things. In any case, all you have to do is call the bank."

"We've done that. Jean-Loup called; they said she had a few hundred thousand francs in the account, and everything seems to be in order."

"Then forget about it. It's just a waste of time. We know what we're looking for."

Forty-five minutes earlier, at exactly ten o'clock, Marseille had telephoned: not a sign of Roger Tramoni, anywhere in the Alpes-Maritimes. The hotel where the waiter in the bar on rue Félix Pyat always stayed on his holiday was in Puget-Théniers, but he had not been there. They had checked every hotel of the same category in the *département*: same result.

Tramoni's description had been passed on to the Sûreté Nationale: medium height, thin, sickly appearance, thirty-seven years old, light-brown hair. As far as Tarquin was concerned, it was the same man who had collected the seven hundred thousand francs at rue Croix-des-Petits-Champs.

"There's no trace of the money yet," Grazzi said.

They had received the serial numbers at about five o'clock the night before. By seven, the printers had turned out thousands of copies of the list, and they were being disseminated wherever the bills might turn up. Fourteen brand-new notes for five hundred new francs each.

"Even with luck, we won't hear anything about them for a day or two," Tarquin said. "This is a madman. He may not even have changed them yet."

"We've notified the mother of the Bombat girl," Grazzi said. "She's coming up from Avignon to identify the body. No one at the office where she worked wanted to do it. She had only been there since yesterday morning and they hardly knew her. In any case, even her mother won't recognize her, the way that bastard left her."

"What else?"

"She left the office about four o'clock, just after she got a telephone call, acting as if she was crazy. Nobody knew why. It's too bad about that child, but we don't know a thing about her. No friends, no acquaintances, no connections at all in Paris. No papers on the body, just like Cabourg. Just the photographs in the room. We found her at eleven o'clock last night. Gabert had finally picked up her trail a quarter of an hour earlier, through a taxi driver. She was killed at about ten or ten-fifteen. One hour, more or less, and she would have been safe. The taxi driver remembered the light-blue coat. It seems she was very pretty, too. He took her to rue du Bac. There was a young boy with her, but we haven't been able to find out a thing about him either."

"What else?"

"Nothing. Unimportant details. The regular customers in the bar in Marseille claim that Roger Tramoni was one of those vicarious gamblers who never gamble themselves. He handled all the tote bets and he made a note of what everyone bet. With the lottery, he wrote down the numbers of every ticket he sold. Whenever somebody won ten thousand francs, he would say, I'm the one who should have had that money; it slipped right through my hands."

Grazzi closed the notebook, saying there was a word for people like that.

"I know," Tarquin said, "masochists."

This morning he had the pulpy, misshapen look of a masochist himself. Grazzi stood up and said, well, when we get our hands on this one, I want to take care of him myself; and since the boss didn't answer him, he said what's the matter, is your liver acting up again, or what?

"It's the gun," Tarquin said. "The woman in the train was strangled, and all the others were shot by a .45 with grooved cartridges – it doesn't fit together. And there's something else: how has he managed to find the people he wanted, faster than we could find them?"

At eleven-thirty that Tuesday morning a sense of triumph took root in the inspectors' office, was relayed from there by telephone to the boss, from him to his boss, and from there to the office of examining magistrate Frégard; Because it was a belated triumph, there was no noise about it, no laughter or joking, as there usually was, and this was a good thing for everyone concerned, because exactly eighteen minutes later, at twelve minutes to noon, nothing remained of this moment of optimism except an acrid taste in the mouth, a bitterness that was best forgotten. For Tarquin, who was a logical man who had always thought that a murder case was a matter of a murderer, a victim, and some witnesses, nothing remained at all.

At eleven-twenty the conductors who had checked the tickets on the Phocéen on Friday night stated that they both remembered a man answering to the description of Roger Tramoni. They had seen him in the corridor of the train.

At eleven-thirty the cashiers in the office of the National Lottery, rue Croix-des-Petits-Champs, formally identified the waiter in the Marseille *bar-tabac* from a photo shown to them by Jouy. They had him now. He was in Paris. It was just a question of hotel registrations, a check of identity cards, the usual.

"He can't have left Paris before eleven o'clock last night; the girl from Avignon wasn't murdered until ten. But we have the Garaudy woman. She must be just as important to him as the others. He must be after her too. And that means he's still here."

This was just about what everyone thought, except perhaps for Tarquin, who was thinking about the gun, and Jean-Loup, who was concentrating on the puzzle and questioning the Garaudy woman at the same time.

At eleven-forty there was a telephone call from the administrative offices of the Paris race tracks. The fourteen new 500-franc notes had been in the cash registers at Vincennes after the Sunday afternoon races.

"For a madman, he's pretty clever," Tarquin said. "He could have changed them, one by one, in department stores, but that would have multiplied the chances of being caught by fourteen, and he would have had to spend some money. But the horses, that's cheap! No reason to spend much of anything; fourteen bets at five new francs each. Ten races, dozens of booths; he never had to go to the same one twice. And so many people that he'd never be recognized. I wouldn't even be surprised if the son of a bitch had won on a couple of them."

Mallet tore up the list of serial numbers and dropped it

in the boss's wastebasket. None of the tellers at Vincennes remembered anything about the man.

It was just then that Pardi came into the office, carrying his camel's-hair overcoat over his arm, dark and impassive, with the slightly timid look he always had. It was eleven forty-six.

"I found him," he said.

"Tramoni?"

"In person."

"Where?"

"In the Seine. They fished him out yesterday afternoon. I found him in Boileau's office, right where I found Cabourg. Boileau is beginning to get fed up. He says it makes him look foolish."

Grazzi had smiled vaguely at Tarquin's last remark, and he had the curious sensation of feeling his own smile fall apart, break into little pieces, and hang from the centre of his mouth, like the paint on the face of a clown.

"Are you crazy?" the boss said.

"Not at all," Pardi's musical voice came back. "He's on the slab; I just saw him. Not a doubt about it. A hole in the head, just like the others."

"When?" Tarquin shouted.

"Don't shout like that. He's been dead since Saturday afternoon. He was in the Seine Saturday night, near Quai de la Râpée. A little girl saw the body come up."

At eleven forty-eight, while Tarquin was trying to light a cigarette, flattened against his chair like a boxer who has taken too much punishment, and Grazzi was still thinking it must be a mistake, a coincidence, one of Pardi's jokes, or something like that, Alloyau came into the office, followed by Gabert.

"She's had it now," Alloyau said. "And I swear I didn't hit her, boss; I just raised my arm to slap a fly."

Tarquin didn't even know who he was talking about.

"Garaudy," Alloyau said. "She wasn't on the train."

"What?"

"No. Her place was reserved, all-right but she didn't use it. She took the noon train. It's one of those stories, and when you take a good look at her, it's easy enough to believe. Her husband was off at work on Friday; he always was, and she knew he wouldn't be back. There was a train at noon, so instead of taking the night train, she took that one. When she got here, she went straight to some other engineer, a friend of her husband's. I have the address. She spent the night with him, at a hotel in rue Gay-Lussac. On Saturday morning he drove her back to the station. She bought a platform ticket, came out with the other passengers from Marseille, fresh as a daisy, and threw her arms around her mother-in-law."

There was a deathly silence in the room when Alloyau finished. He had been pleased with himself, thinking he had succeeded in his job, and now he didn't know what to think.

"She couldn't admit she wasn't on the train, don't you see?" he said feebly. "She says her whole life is ruined. She says I don't know her mother-in-law, I don't know that family. She's crying again . . ."

"Are you going to shut up?"

It was Grazzi who said it, standing beside the boss's desk with his notebook in his hand, not daring to look down at it, or put it back in his pocket, or draw attention to it in any way, that stupid, useless notebook.

The boss stood up, unlit cigarette drooping from his lips,

put his hand on Grazzi's arm, and said well, he was going to make up some kind of a report, there was no point in Grazzi worrying this way; if the whole thing was shot, it was shot. They had a score to settle with this son of a something or other, he and Grazzi did, and one of these days they would settle it.

"For the next few days we'll just try to walk down the corridors without being noticed. We won't give up; we'll just make ourselves very small. We had a case with a victim, a murderer, and some witnesses. Now, we don't have our murderer, and we don't have any witnesses. Victims can't talk, and I'm going to do the same thing; I'm going to keep my mouth shut and hide."

He put on his overcoat and said, I'll be back at two o'clock, we'll see what we have left, what we can do.

A policeman was standing on the threshold, trying to attract Grazzi's attention. In vain, because Grazzi was looking at the boss, and the boss never looked at anyone.

"Monsieur Grazziano," the policeman said. "There's a girl in the waiting room who says her name is Bombat. She wants to see you, and no one else."

All Grazzi heard was the boss saying, after all, if that female didn't occupy the berth, someone else must have, because there was someone there. "That's reasonable, isn't it?"

Grazzi put the useless notebook in the inside pocket of his coat, looking at the boss, thinking, why is it that he doesn't annoy me so much today, why should I be thinking he's my friend? He nodded to the policeman and said, all-right, all-right, I'm coming, what did you say her name was?

Berth 000

"Grazzi? Jouy here. There's a call for you, from Marseille."

"Who is it?"

"I don't know. The switchboard just said he asked for you."

"Take it for me, will you? I'm busy with the girl."

"He asked for you."

"Will you just do as I say, please?"

"Georges? Jouy again. Grazzi's busy. What does that guy from Marseille want?"

"Don't ask me. All I could hear was God damn it. It sounded like a kid. He said he only had enough money to pay for the first three minutes. He wants Grazzi to call him back. He's waiting in the bar in Marseille. He said Grazzi would understand."

"Put him on here."

"I can't. He's already hung up."

"Jouy? Grazzi here. What was all that about the call from Marseille?"

"Just now? The switchboard operator thought it was some kid. He wants you to call him back; said he would wait in the bar, that you would understand. Do you?"

184

"Did he leave his name?"

"No. I didn't even talk to him. He didn't have any money, and had to hang up."

"How long ago?

"Ten, fifteen minutes."

"Look – I'm in the boss's office with the girl. Call that bar on rue Félix Pyat in Marseille and put the call in here. As soon as I have it, call the Préfecture in Marseille yourself, and tell them to send someone there and not to let him get away after I talk to him. Then find Pardi and tell him to get the boss back here as fast as possible."

"Have you got something?"

"Will you just do as I say, please?"

"Hello. This is Inspector Grazziano. Are you Daniel?"

"Yes. Can you hear me?"

"What the devil are you doing in Marseille?"

"That would take too long to explain. Where is Bambi?"

"Who?"

"Mademoiselle Bombat. Benjamine Bombat. I know where you can find her."

'You do, eh? Well, so do I. What are you doing in that bar?"

"You know where she is?"

"She's right here."

"She's with you?"

"Yes, she's with me. And stop shouting. What are you doing in that bar?"

"I told you; it would take a long time to explain."

"I have plenty of time, you idiot! And we're paying for the call! I thought you went home, to Nice."

"You mean you know who I am?"

"I'd have to be deaf not to know! I've heard nothing but you and all your nonsense for the last three quarters of an hour."

"Is she all-right?"

"She's perfectly all-right. She's sitting on the other side of the desk, she has her head in her hands, and she's weeping all over the commissioner's files. Nothing can happen to her now! You're the one I'm worried about, you little fool! Now, are you going to tell me what you're doing in Marseille – yes or no?"

"It's because of the strike."

"What strike?"

"The rail workers' strike, of course."

"What day is today?"

"Tuesday. Why?"

"I wasn't talking to you! And stop shouting. All-right, so the strike is on. Now, will you please tell me, very calmly, what you are doing in Marseille? Without shouting."

"I'm not shouting. I'm in Marseille because I can't go any further, because of the strike."

"The train you took last night arrived in Nice more than five hours ago. Are you trying to make fun of me?"

"No. You see, I didn't come to Marseille on that train. I got off it at Dijon."

"Why?"

"You wouldn't understand."

"Damn it, will you answer my questions? Then you'll see whether or not I understand. Did you plan to take a train back here?"

"Is that what she thought?"

"Yes, that's what she thought! And when she got home last night, that's what she thought you had done. There was a light in her room. But it wasn't you who was waiting for her, it was a poor girl who had brought back her handbag and been welcomed by a bullet in the head! We're not playing games any more! This is for real! Now do you understand?"

"Did they kill someone else?"

"Yes, they killed someone else. Sandrine. Why do you say 'they'?"

"Because there are two of them."

"Did you know that last night, when you saw her at the station? Is that what you meant when you said you understood?"

"I didn't really understand anything, then."

"You understood that they were going to kill someone else! You said so!"

"I meant myself. I thought they were after me!"

"Did you know who it was?"

"No. It wasn't until I saw the papers this morning, at the station in Marseille, that I understood. I should have known before this, but so should you."

"I won't argue that you're better informed than we are; that's exactly why I'm worried about you, you fool. Why didn't you come and tell us everything you knew right away?"

"I didn't want any trouble. I saw a dead woman, that's all. Someone else would find her, a few minutes later. I didn't want any trouble. It was none of my business."

"I'm not talking about Saturday. I'm talking about last night, when you knew a lot of things we needed to know, and you decided to run home to papa, instead of coming here."

"I didn't know they had killed anyone else. I knew they were looking for me, that's all. I thought if I got away from her, Bambi wouldn't be in any danger; that's why I left. But then I started thinking about it in the train. I was afraid they might find her while they were looking for me, and then they wouldn't dare let her go. So I decided to come back. But there was no train from Dijon to Paris until this morning, and this morning the strike was going to be on. So I took another train to go on to Nice, because I thought my father would know what to do. He's a lawyer."

"I know. So, you started back to Nice again. Why did you get off at Marseille?"

"Because I saw the newspapers in the station, when the train stopped here. That's when I really understood. Last night I didn't know anything about the lottery ticket, or the serial numbers on the money. Or the other murders."

"You followed Cabourg, Saturday night. Didn't you know that he had been killed?"

"No, of course not! I followed Cabourg, then I followed the police – you and that young one who wears a duffel coat – and then I followed Grandin. Don't you understand? I was going from one to the other; it was a regular merry-go-round."

"A what?"

"A merry-go-round. You know, those toys you wind up, with animals that turn around and look as if they're chasing each other. A carousel. I was running after someone, and he was running after me. At least that's what I thought, but I was wrong. When I read the paper this morning, I realized that the animals were off the track – one of them was going in the opposite direction. So I came to this bar, to see if I was wrong again. But I wasn't, this time. I found out that you were looking for the waiter,

Roger Tramoni, which is just what I thought would have happened. Except that Roger Tramoni is probably dead, and you're wasting your time."

"We know that."

"Is he dead?"

"He's dead. He's been dead since Saturday. They found him in the Seine. Why did you follow me? And why did you follow Grandin?"

"Where is Bambi?"

"I told you – right here with me! Damn it, will you listen to me?"

"Who's with you? Where are you?"

"What do you mean, where am I?"

"I'm just thinking of one thing! If he made a mistake last night, and killed Sandrine because he thought she was Bambi, he knows who Bambi is now!"

"How?"

"Where are you?"

"In the commissioner's office! Quai des Orfèvres! How could she be in any danger here?"

"I don't know. He's crazy."

"Who? Grandin?"

"No. The other one."

"Listen to me, you little __ ."

"Hello? Inspector Grazziano?"

"Yes."

"Hello! Can you hear me?"

"Yes. Listen, son; I've got to hang up. Stay right where you are. I'll call you back. Don't move from there."

"Inspector!"

"Yes."

"You understand, now?"

"Yes."

"Is he there?"

"Yes."

"Can he hear me?"

"Yes."

"Mallet? Grazzi. Well?"

"I don't know what to think. The bank says they told him all about it, when he called this morning about the chequebook."

"Told him about what?"

"Eliane Darrès wrote a check for six million francs last week. Listen, Grazzi __ ."

"When was it cashed?"

"Friday, at eleven o'clock."

"Who was it made out to?"

"Alphonse Rahis. He identified himself with a driver's licence – a Paris one. I have the number. Jouy is checking it now. From the bank's description of him, it could be Grandin. Are you sure this isn't all some sort of hoax?"

"I'm not sure of anything."

"Grazzi? Jouy here. The only Alphonse Rahis I could find at the licence bureau died two years ago, in prison. Embezzlement and cirrhosis of the liver."

"That fits. He could have lifted the driver's licence from a file somewhere, and changed the photo."

"Does the boss know about it?"

"He's just come in. Judge Frégard too."

"Do they believe it?"

"They're beginning to."

* * *

"Inspector Grazziano?"

"Yes. Now listen to me carefully, son. I'm going to ask the questions, from now on, and you're going to answer me as precisely as possible. Do you understand?"

"How did you guess what I meant?"

"I didn't guess anything. You were afraid, for Bambi. I asked myself why you should be afraid. I thought about a gun, and about a chequebook that had disappeared. And about some things Bambi had told me. And the way someone managed to get there before I did every time. Now you've got to listen to me. I'm sitting at my boss's desk, and he's sitting beside me, listening on another phone. There are two other inspectors, looking at me as if I was crazy. You understand? If you're wrong, it's a very serious matter for everyone."

"I'm not wrong."

"All-right. Now tell me everything you did after you got off the train, after you went back for your suitcase. You went to rue du Bac with Bambi. Begin with that."

"Just tell me where he is, first."

"He's in another office. The police have gone to pick up Grandin."

"What did he say?"

"He said it was absurd."

"What is his name?"

"Gabert. Jean-Loup Gabert."

"He wears a duffel coat, has wavy blond hair and girlish manners? He's the one who was with you?"

"Yes, he was with me. When did you begin following us? Saturday, about two or three o'clock?"

"I don't know exactly. I had lunch with Bambi. Then I left her and went back to Gare de Lyon. I left my scarf in

191

the compartment next to the one we were in. It was my mother's, printed with a view of Nice. I was worried about it, because I was afraid you might be able to trace it to me. But in the end, I didn't dare go and ask about it."

"Wait a second."

"What are you doing? Checking on the scarf?"

"Yes. Go ahead. What did you think had happened, then?"

"That you had caught the murderer in the act. I didn't know how, but that was the impression I had. I thought it was the sick man I had seen in the corridor. I was right about that; he had been arrested in the compartment. But it was Gabert who arrested him."

"All-right; let's keep things in order. After Gare de Lyon, you came to Quai des Orfèvres; right?"

"Yes. I walked for a long time, and then I took a bus. I saw you come out with Gabert. I didn't know who you were, then, but you stopped to talk to someone and I heard you say something about a murder and the station, so I listened. I heard you say you were going to rue Duperré. I thought of talking to you then, but before I could make up my mind you got into a car and left. So I went to rue Duperré too. I didn't know the number of the building, but I saw the police car parked in the street. I looked in some of the buildings, but I didn't even know what I was looking for. I waited for you to come out, but while I was waiting I had a better idea. I thought about Cabourg, and decided to try to find him."

"Why?"

"I don't know exactly. He had had an argument with the woman on the train, and then I found her dead. I was confused, but I thought I ought to do something. Do you understand? That was the only thing I really knew. I had heard him talking to her about his work, about Progine. I decided to try and find him; but I wasn't sure whether his name was Labour or Cabour. I didn't pay much attention on the train. When I telephoned, I just said, 'Monsieur Aour.'"

"You telephoned Progine?"

"Yes. I went into a café on rue Duperré and looked it up in the telephone book. There were several addresses for Progine. I called the main office, and then started on the branches. At the third one, Alésia something-or-other, I found him. I said I was a customer, making up my Christmas list."

"I know. You got his address. Go ahead."

"I told myself I had plenty of time, so I walked for a while, and then I took another bus to where he lived. He wasn't home yet, so I waited on the pavement. I bought *France-Soir*, and saw the list of passengers. Then I knew I had been wrong that morning, and you hadn't arrested the murderer. I was hungry, so I went into a restaurant in his building to get something to eat. All of a sudden, while I was eating, I saw Cabourg, looking in the window. Then he went away again. By the time I paid the bill and got out of there, he was already a block away. And there was someone following him. The policeman I had seen with you, the one in the duffel coat. Right after that, Cabourg began to run."

"What time was it?"

"Fairly late. About nine o'clock, I guess."

"Where did you follow them to?"

"I didn't follow them. Cabourg got into a taxi in front of the station. I don't know which station; the one that's near where he lives. Paris is full of stations."

"Gare de l'Est. So you lost him there?"

"I didn't lose him. He took a taxi, and Gabert took another one, following him. As far as I was concerned, that was all there was to it. The police knew who he was, and were after him. Besides, I didn't have any more money. Steaks are expensive in Paris. I went back to Bambi's. There was a note on the door, so I walked over to Sandrine's."

"All-right. I know what you did the next morning, Bambi has already told me. You came to Quai des Orfèvres first; you still couldn't make up your mind about coming in. Then you saw Gabert go out, about eleven o'clock."

"Yes. He got in a taxi."

"And went to rue La Fontaine to question Madame Garaudy. You took a taxi and followed him. Why?"

"Because I had been thinking about it, and I knew there was something wrong. Cabourg couldn't be the murderer. In the first place, I saw him leave the station while I was waiting for Bambi by the exit. In the second place, he wasn't one of the two men I had heard in the compartment. I was sure that the murderer was the man I saw in the corridor, the sick one, and that you were making a mistake."

"So you and Bambi followed Gabert?"

"Yes. He went to rue Duperré first. I got out of the taxi, but I didn't have time to follow him and see where he went. He came out again almost immediately."

"What did you think, then?"

"Nothing. I thought there was probably some reason for him to stop by there. We just went on following him. He went to rue La Fontaine. There was a *bar-tabac* across from the house, and we waited in there. He came in later and made a telephone call. What I thought then, and told Bambi, was that you were wrong about everything. I saw the name Garaudy on the door of the house in rue La Fontaine, and it was one of the names in the paper, so I knew that was who he had gone to see. But whoever Garaudy is, he couldn't have been in the compartment, because I was in that berth."

"We know that now. Go ahead."

"We followed Gabert again. He went back to rue Duperré. Bambi and I followed him into the building, and we had to hide in a corner, because he was coming down the stairs with a boy with dark hair. I learned later that it was Eric Grandin, Georgette Thomas' friend."

"All-right, Bambi told me about that. They separated on the street, and you thought Gabert was doing his job, so you followed him again. What time was it?"

"About one o'clock. He took another taxi, and went to Clichy. Bambi was beginning to get angry, because she had spent a lot of money on taxis, and she couldn't see what it was all about."

"And that took you to Rivolani's?"

"Yes. The policeman in the duffel coat went into a house in a dead end. We waited about a quarter of an hour, and then he came out and went to look at the garages, and got in another taxi."

"You lost him then. You thought he was going back to the Quai, or to question another witness, and gave up following him. Is that right?"

"Yes. We had lunch in Clichy, and looked in the telephone book and found the address of the actress."

"So you went to the Trocadéro?"

"Yes."

"You had really made up your mind to play detective by this time, hadn't you?"

"Yes. I thought you were making a mistake."

"When did you go to Vincennes?"

"Before the Trocadéro. That's right – we went to Vincennes first. We did so much, I got it confused."

"Why did you go there?"

"While we were hiding in the staircase, at rue Duperré, I heard Grandin talking as they went down. It sounded like something dangerous and important – as if Grandin was doing something to help the police. Gabert was the police after all. He said he would be at Vincennes in time for the first race, and would stay there. I left Bambi at the entrance, when we got to Vincennes, so we would only have to pay for one ticket. I found Grandin at the betting booths."

"What was he doing?"

"Betting. I waited awhile, thinking something was going to happen, but nothing did. Grandin just went back to the booths and made another bet. So I left."

"You little idiot. Suppose he had seen you, and realized you were following him?"

"I know. But I never got close to him, and there were a lot of people. I didn't know anything about the lottery or the new notes. This morning, I understood what he was doing."

"Go on. You went to the Trocadéro after that?"

"Yes. I saw you with Gabert. You were coming out of the actress' house. Gabert went back in, and you waited for him in the car. Bambi was in a tearoom; she was exhausted."

"So you followed me?"

"No. You left with Gabert, and Bambi was about to get hysterical, so I let it drop. We walked down to the *quais*, and then went to a restaurant for dinner. It was very noisy."

"What about the next day? Yesterday – Monday."

"Bambi went to the office in the morning. I went back to the Trocadéro, to talk to the actress."

"Why?"

"I was going to explain what I knew to her, and see what she could tell me. But when I got to the house, there were a lot of policemen in front of the door. I saw Gabert arrive; he was running. I thought you had arrested Eliane Darrès."

"You think that's the way we arrest people? With a flock of policemen around the door?"

"If the number of them waiting for me in this bar is any sample, yes! Are you going to put me in prison?"

"No. Are they there now?"

"Yes, they're here."

"Don't worry about that. Tell me what you learned yesterday afternoon, and then I'll explain what you should do."

"Explain first, and I'll tell you the rest afterwards. If you're going to arrest me, I won't say anything more until my father is here."

"Look, son, Grandin is being brought in now. They're questioning Gabert in the next office, and he denies everything."

"Where is Bambi?"

"In a corner of the room where I am. She has an enormous ham sandwich in her hands, and she's eating. That's what you should do, too. You've told me almost enough, but not quite. I have a couple more things to ask, and then you're going to let me talk to the officer in charge of those men. After I've talked to him, you're going to behave yourself and go with him wherever he takes you. I'll call you again there. Do you understand?"

"All-right. But I think you should notify my father anyway."

"We did that a long time ago. Now, what about yesterday afternoon?"

"Bambi went back to the office after lunch. I didn't have the key, so I left the door to her room open. It was about ten minutes to two, I suppose, because she had to be back at two-fifteen. I went to rue Duperré."

"Why?"

"Because I had seen Grandin that morning, in front of Eliane Darrès' house. And it was funny, in a way, because he was hiding too, just as I was. He was in a car, a Dauphine, parked a little way down the street. I think now that Gabert got out of that car when he arrived there."

"Let's get back to rue Duperré."

"All-right. I went upstairs. You were in Grandin's room. I could hear your voice on the landing, without getting too close to the door. You were saying, 'Did you ever hear her mention anyone named Rivolani, or Eliane Darrès?' He said no. I didn't understand anything more. When you came out, I just barely had time to go down a few steps. You would have heard me if I had gone down all the way in front of you, so I turned around and came back up. You asked me if I was a friend of Grandin's."

"That was you – the boy in the raincoat?"

"Yes. I was afraid you might have seen me at Quai des Orfèvres, or in front of the actress' house, and would recognize me, but you didn't. In any case, you had given me an idea. I went to see Grandin. I told him I was a student at the Sorbonne, and wanted to start a students' newspaper. We talked for a while, and I could see that he was afraid of something. I stayed about ten minutes, asking him questions about his life as a student, and what he planned to do. I didn't dare talk about the murder; I was frightened myself. But I thought if I said something about trains, it would be natural for him to tell me about what had happened to one of his friends on a train."

"Did you try it?"

"Yes. But he didn't tell me anything. On the contrary, after that he began asking me questions. Where I came from, who I was, how I knew his address, where I lived. I was scared. I didn't really know why, but I realized a few minutes later, when I got out of the bus to go back to Bambi's. The Dauphine was following me. I got on another bus, and then took the metro. I went back to Bambi's, picked up my suitcase, and got away from rue du Bac as fast as I could. I telephoned Bambi from a café in the Latin Quarter. I told her I was in Clichy, but I wasn't. I didn't want her to know where I was."

"All-right, son. Let me talk to the officer in charge now."

"Okay. You don't want to know the rest – how I worked it out when I saw the paper this morning?"

"I think I understand myself, now. I'll call you back in a little while. You go with the officer, and don't worry."

"Judge Frégard? Commissioner Tarquin speaking."

"Have they talked yet?"

"No, but Grandin won't hold out much longer. We've got the cheque, and the teller at the bank has positively identified him as the man who cashed it, under the name of Alphonse Rahis. Eliane Darrès' signature is a good forgery – he must have worked on that – but the endorsement is his handwriting. He tried to disguise it, of course, but it isn't a good job."

"What about the search of Gabert's apartment?"

"Nothing. It's a regular museum of firearms, but there's no sign of the gun we're looking for, or of the money. Funny – we found out that he's an orphan who was brought up by an aunt in the provinces. I don't know why, but everyone here thought he was the son of some big shot."

"Who's questioning him?"

"Grazzi. He knows Gabert, and he knows his profession; he's a good man. We took him to an office across the street; it's more private. This place is lousy with reporters."

"I'll put him on, Inspector Grazziano. He's perfectly all-right. He's been eating all afternoon."

"Daniel?"

"Yes, inspector. Is Bambi all-right?"

"She went to her office, but she's coming back here tonight. I'm going to need you, too; I'm trying to find some way to get you here."

"Have they confessed yet?"

"No. Grandin is being questioned, and so is Gabert. I'm going to talk to him myself in a few minutes, but there were one or two things I wanted to ask you first. Can you hear me?"

"Yes, inspector, very well."

"Good. I don't understand why Gabert let the actress leave the station, or why he had decided to kill her on the train. Do you know anything about that?"

"The actress – Eliane Darrès? I didn't know who it was they really wanted to kill. When I saw the papers this morning, I thought it must be Eliane Darrès – they couldn't have had any reason to kill Rivolani or Cabourg –

but I wasn't sure. But in any case, they never meant to kill her on the train."

"Well, who did he mean to kill? Georgette Thomas?"

"No! Georgette Thomas was in it with them! Don't you understand at all? It was Bambi they meant to kill."

"Bambi? What in God's name does she have to do with it?"

"Nothing. That's just it; it didn't matter. It could have been Bambi, or anyone else in the compartment – except Eliane Darrès. Georgette Thomas was supposed to keep one of them in the compartment with her. Gabert was supposed to get on the train and kill whoever it was."

"But why?"

"That was the whole plan! What did you do, when you found Georgette Thomas? You started an investigation into the murder of Georgette Thomas. Then someone in the same compartment gets murdered, and you thought it was a question of eliminating a witness to her murder. Gabert knew what you would think, so he reversed the roles! Anyone at all could have been the original victim. The person they were really after becomes a witness, just because she was in the same compartment; you wouldn't even look for another motive. Especially because Gabert wouldn't be satisfied with killing just her; he'd kill one or two others, too – Cabourg and Rivolani – to be sure you thought it was all a business of getting rid of the witnesses. Do you understand?"

"I think I do, now, yes. But how did you work it out?"

"It was a lot of things. None of them made any sense until I saw the papers today, and then they all fell together. Bambi told me how Georgette Thomas had looked at her, and how she tried to keep her in the compartment. Grandin knew Georgette Thomas, and he knew Gabert too. But the main thing was, when I heard Gabert talking to Grandin on the staircase, I was sure he was the man I had heard in the compartment, talking to the sick man, Tramoni. I recognized his voice. He talked to Grandin the same way he did to Tramoni, as if he were giving orders. There were other things too, little things. I knew Rivolani couldn't have been a witness to anything, because I had heard him snoring."

"Then it wasn't Gabert who killed Georgette Thomas? It was Tramoni."

"Of course. She was strangled – by an amateur, the paper said – and all the others were shot. It wasn't part of the plan for Georgette Thomas to be killed; but it wasn't part of the plan for her to win the lottery and be followed by Tramoni. When Gabert arrived – to kill someone else – he found Georgette Thomas dead and Tramoni in the compartment. That's when I heard them. But what could he do? He went ahead with the plan. He just substituted Georgette Thomas for Bambi. The only thing I still don't know is why they wanted to kill Eliane Darrès. Do you?"

"They cashed a forged check for six million francs on Eliane Darrès' account last Friday."

"Oh. You sound tired, inspector."

"I am. Very tired. This whole thing is terrible."

"I know. Rivolani, Cabourg, and maybe Bambi . . ."

"That's terrible, but it's not what I meant. How old are you?"

"Sixteen. Why?"

"That's what's terrible."

* * *

"Grazzi? Tarquin. Forget about him and come back here."

"Is Grandin going to talk?"

"Yes."

"What did you do?"

"I showed him some pictures of his Georgette. Dead."

This Is the Way It Ended

*Transcript of interrogation of Charles (Eric) Grandin,
conducted by Commissioner Tarquin and
Inspector Grazziano*

Question: You told us that you have known Jean-Loup
Gabert for some time. When did you introduce him to
Georgette Thomas?

Answer: About two months ago. We had dinner together,
in a restaurant in Les Halles.

Q. When did you decide to kill Eliane Darrès?

A. It didn't happen like that. We didn't just decide on it
all at once. We saw each other frequently, and Jean-Loup
talked about his work and the people he worked with. We
tried to work out something that would be a perfect crime,
but we weren't thinking of anyone in particular. Jean-Loup
and I used to laugh at Georgette, because she was so naïve
she would have been caught in a minute. Then, one day,
I mentioned Eliane, because she had given me a key to her
apartment and I knew she had money.

Q. How long had it been since you had last seen Eliane
Darrès?

A. Several months. I knew she had been looking for me,
in a café on Place Danton where I first met her, but I didn't
go there any more.

Q. Whose idea was it, originally?

A. It was all three of us. It was a game; each of us put in an idea, a new angle. Then Jean-Loup told me that it would work; we would be fools if we didn't use it. When I realized that he was serious about it, I got frightened. I talked to Georgette, but she said, "There's no harm in listening to him; that doesn't involve us in anything." One night we went to his apartment and he showed us his collection of guns. He said he had a silencer. There wouldn't be any problem, because he would always know what the police were doing. He would make a point of being on duty when the murder was reported, and after that he would know what was happening, even if he wasn't assigned to the case himself.

Q. Then the idea of killing someone else, *before* you killed Eliane Darrès, was his?

A. He said that the only perfect crime was a crime that had no motive. If there was an investigation of a murder, and two people who might have been witnesses to that murder were killed, the police would think it was all part of the original murder. So you could kill the person you really wanted to kill without running any risk at all. He said he knew the people he worked with. They would link the two later murders to the first. And the first one would be the one that had no motive.

Q. In other words, Gabert actually planned three murders? Didn't the thought of that frighten you?

A. I don't know. I didn't think it was real; it was still a game to me. It was Georgette who got frightened. I talked to her about it that night, after we left Jean-Loup. I thought he was right, but she was frightened. Besides, as soon as you accept the idea of killing someone, the number of people you kill becomes unimportant. I still think that.

Q. In spite of Rivolani, and the girl, Sandrine?

A. At the time, I didn't know who it would be. Even now when I say the number is unimportant, it's because it's an abstract thing to me; I can't see their faces. I never saw Rivolani, Cabourg, or the girl. That's probably why Georgette and I never really thought it was true.

Q. When did you decide to carry out the plan?

A. When I learned that Eliane was going to Aix-en-Provence to make a film.

Q. When did you learn that?

A. About two days before she left – the day I found the chequebook in her apartment. I'd been watching the apartment for a couple of weeks. When she went out, I used the key she gave me, and went in to look around. I didn't disturb anything. I was just looking for the chequebook to see how much money she had in the bank, but she never left it. But on that day she must have gone out in a hurry, because she left her handbag. The chequebook was in it, and a letter telling her she had been hired and to come to Aix. I took a cheque from the middle of the book and cut out the stub with a razor blade, so she wouldn't notice it was missing. When the police investigated, after she was dead, Jean-Loup was going to make sure the chequebook wasn't found.

Q. When did you make out the cheque?

A. I didn't do that; Georgette did. She was very good at copying other people's signatures. I found an old social-security form in Eliane's desk; she copied it from that.

Q. And what about cashing the cheque?

A. Jean-Loup arranged to get the list of reservations on the trains from Marseille and Nice. As soon as we knew when Eliane was coming back to Paris, I was to go to the bank. Jean-Loup had got me a driver's licence in the name of Rahis, for identification, and the cheque was made out to him. We changed the photograph on it. I had to wait a long time at the bank, but they didn't ask any questions.

Q. And Georgette Thomas was to be told, in Marseille, when Eliane Darrès was leaving, and get a berth in the same compartment?

A. Not necessarily the same compartment. That might have been difficult, and Jean-Loup didn't think it was important. She was just supposed to be on the same train.

Q. Do you think she tried to get a berth in that compartment deliberately?

A. Yes. She wanted to stop the whole thing, when she learned she had won a prize in the lottery. She forgot that on Friday I had already cashed the cheque. And I didn't get her telegram until late on Friday.

Q. Why would she have tried to stop you? Because she had seven hundred thousand francs, instead of six million?

A. You didn't know Georgette. If she had won only half of that, a quarter of it, she would have taken it as a sign from heaven. She never won at anything.

Q. Do you remember what she said in the telegram?

A. Yes. "Project impossible. Will explain. Georgette." I thought she was frightened. But it didn't matter, then; I didn't get the telegram until after I had been to the bank on Friday.

Q. But she must have sent it on Thursday, as soon as she knew about the lottery. We can check on that.

A. That's another thing I don't understand myself. If she had sent it to me at home, I would have got it on Thursday. The concierge would have taken it for me, even if I hadn't been there myself. But she sent it to a café near my school —

a place I always get messages, and leave them for my friends. I didn't go there until Friday evening.

Q. Is that where you left the money? And the gun?

A. Yes. In a suitcase of Jean-Loup's.

Q. Let's admit that Georgette Thomas was worried, and wanted to stop the whole thing, and that's why she got a berth in the same compartment with Eliane Darrès. Did you know that before the train arrived?

A. I didn't, but Jean-Loup did. He had the reservation lists. I think that's why she did it. She knew he would know, and she thought that if he knew she was in the same compartment, he wouldn't dare go ahead. We never planned for her to be questioned as a witness.

Q. But she did try to keep the girl from Avignon. How do you explain that?

A. I can't. Georgette was like that. I think that, at the last minute, she remembered the way Jean-Loup had laughed at her, and said she was the type to be caught immediately. She was afraid we would all be caught, unless she went ahead with her part of the plan.

Q. When did you learn that she had been killed?

A. When I went to Jean-Loup's apartment, Saturday morning at eleven o'clock. It was part of the plan that we would all meet there. Jean-Loup had just come back from Gare de Lyon, after the initial police investigation. He had brought Tramoni there earlier, and left him locked in the apartment. He told me what had happened, and said there would just be the two of us to share the money now. I was stunned; I didn't know what was happening any more.

Q. How did Gabert get Tramoni from the station to his apartment?

A. He had Georgette's car. He had arrested Tramoni, and told him that if he didn't make any trouble, and split the money with him, he would see to it that he got away. Tramoni was a very stupid man.

Q. When did you kill him?

A. When we got back from rue Croix-des-Petits-Champs. Jean-Loup and I drove him there, and waited outside while he went in and redeemed the lottery ticket. I didn't even know Jean-Loup was planning to kill him. But when we got back to his apartment, he took out the gun and the silencer. Tramoni was counting the money again; he never knew what was happening. We put the body under the bed, and about two or three o'clock in the morning we carried it down and put it in the car. We dropped him in the Seine near Quai de la Râpée.

Q. And after that you killed Eliane Darrès, because the cheque had already been cashed, and you had to get her out of the way before she discovered it. But what about Cabourg and Rivolani?

A. At first Jean-Loup said we would just go ahead with the original plan. Someone else would have to be killed, to throw you off the track. But then he admitted to me that he had been mistaken; something had gone wrong.

Q. He had realized that someone had heard him talking to Tramoni? That there had been someone in the next compartment?

A. Yes. He knew it must have been one of the passengers in the compartment with Georgette, but he didn't know which one. He realized it when he went back to Gare de Lyon with you, for the initial investigation. He noticed right away that there was only one suitcase in the compartment then, but there had been two when he was in there earlier, with Tramoni. He thought they were both Georgette's. If someone had gone into the compartment before the guard found the body, that someone might have seen him. And it must have been one of the other passengers, because he had taken the suitcase.

Q. Was that all?

A. No. There was something else he didn't understand. Georgette had had an argument with Cabourg on the train. Tramoni told us about it. Then Cabourg telephoned you that night, and gave you his address. Jean-Loup said he didn't want to run the risk of letting you talk to him again. He followed him that night, and shot him. I didn't know about it until the next day.

Q. Whose idea was it to kill Eliane Darrès in the lift?

A. Mine. One night while I was waiting for her on the landing – before she gave me the key – I kept opening and closing the door so the lift wouldn't work properly, as a joke. I told Jean-Loup about it.

Q. But it wasn't you who killed Eliane Darrès?

A. I didn't kill anyone. I was frightened, but I didn't know how to stop it. Jean-Loup said it had to be done. After Tramoni, all he could think about was killing. He said it was easy, after you had once begun. I didn't even know about Rivolani's murder until I saw the papers this morning. And you told me about the girl; I didn't know he had killed her either.

Q. How long had Gabert known that Madame Garaudy wasn't on the train?

A. Right from the beginning. He's the one who spoke to the conductors for you, the first day. They check off the names of the passengers on a list, and they hadn't checked Madame Garaudy. He knew when he questioned her that she was lying, but since she insisted she had been on the train, he thought it would just confuse you more.

Q. But Gabert also knew that someone had actually occupied her berth. Didn't that worry him?

A. Yes. There were a lot of things that worried him. Tramoni had done a lot of stupid things. Instead of trying to be as inconspicuous as possible, he had stood around in the corridors most of the night. Everyone on the train must have seen him. Then, he found the lottery ticket in an empty aspirin tube in Georgette's pocket. The other people in the compartment all remembered that Georgette had taken the tube from her suitcase, but apparently never took the aspirin. She probably just wanted to keep the ticket where she knew it would be safe; she was like that. But instead of keeping the tube, or throwing it away, Tramoni put it back in her handbag. Jean-Loup said it was stupid mistakes like that that got people caught.

Q. Did Tramoni tell you how he happened to know about the seven hundred thousand francs?

A. Yes. He was a miserable little man. When I first saw him, in Jean-Loup's apartment, he was shaking like a leaf. He told us that all he wanted was to get the ticket from her, but she started to scream, and he got panicky. He wrote down the numbers of every ticket he sold in the bar. She had been in there the day after the draw, and since she didn't say anything about having won, he thought she hadn't seen the paper and didn't know. He took his holiday and followed her to Paris. I don't know how he thought he could get away with it. I think he was crazy.

Q. And how did you think you could get away with all this?

A. I don't know that either. I trusted Jean-Loup. When

the three of us talked about it, it all seemed so simple. I never even thought about the people. I had never had a gun in my hand, until he showed us his.

Q. Then why do you hate him now?

A. I don't hate him.

Q. Then why are you accusing him of responsibility for the whole plan?

A. Because it had to be stopped. All of this killing wouldn't change anything now. The cheque was already cashed when he got on the train. If Tramoni hadn't already done it, and there had been no one else in the compartment, he would have killed Georgette. I'm sure of that. *He had to kill someone.* He probably would have killed me before it was over.

Q. What were the real reasons behind the whole plan?

A. I don't understand what you mean.

Q. Why did you decide to do it in the first place?

A. I don't know. We were going to go to South Africa or Australia. I would have gone first, with Eliane's money, and then Georgette would come and join me. Jean-Loup, too, maybe. I don't know. We would have done something. We would have gone away.

Inspector Grazziano was sitting at the desk in the boss's office, alone, staring at the last two cartridges from the barrel of a Smith and Wesson revolver lying in the palm of his right hand. He was thinking of his son, Dino, three years and seven months old, lying in bed asleep, with his little fists clenched tight around the pillow, the way he always slept. When the boss came in, Grazzi stood the cartridges carefully in the centre of the desk, directly in front of him.

Tarquin looked at them, and then at Grazzi, closed the door, dropped some typewritten papers he had been carrying on the desk, and said, well Mister Holmes, how goes it now, I was supposed to go to a movie with my wife tonight, but it's too late now. He took a cigarette from his pocket, said that that pighead Frégard had calmed down at last, give me a light, please, someone is always stealing my matches.

The door opened again, and Mallet put his head into the office to say that the Bombat girl was waiting in the corridor.

"Damn it," Grazzi said, "I almost forgot."

He picked up the telephone and asked for Marseille. He told the boss he would be out of his way in a minute, he was just arranging to bring the boy back to Paris. The pretty blonde girl came in, hesitantly, and the boss said, come in, come in, child, sit down here, how is the job going?

She smiled timidly, but didn't answer. She was standing in front of the desk, her face looking a trifle pale in the glare from the lamp. Grazzi looked at her as he spoke into the phone.

"Daniel? Listen, son. It's seven o'clock now. In an hour, someone will drive you to the airport there. I've talked to your father about it. An army plane will fly you up here, and I'll meet you at Le Bourget."

"What time will I get there?"

"About eleven o'clock. I've arranged for a place for you to stay tonight, and your father is going to join you here tomorrow."

"To defend me?"

"No. To bring you some clean clothes. You'll probably have to see Gabert and Grandin, you know."

"I can think of someone else I'd rather see."

"I'll give you fifteen seconds to talk to her."

The girl took the receiver from his hand, standing very straight in her blue coat, her blonde hair shining in the light from the lamp, and the boss inhaled deeply on his cigarette, dropping ash on his waistcoat, his face shining with sweat, as usual, looking tired.

Grazzi walked around the desk. He could hear the murmur of the boy's voice from the telephone. Mademoiselle Benjamine Bombat turned around, so they couldn't see her face, not speaking, just nodding silently, yes, yes, yes. The boy was saying, can you hear me, hello, they're going to bring me back to Paris, I'll see you again, I'll see you tonight, hello, can you hear me, why don't you say something, Bambi? He was saying, Bambi, my little Bambi, and without a word, just by the movement of her head, with her blonde hair shining in the light from the lamp, she was saying, yes, yes, yes.

A VERY LONG ENGAGEMENT

Winner of the Prix Interallié

"Diabolically clever . . . The reader is alternately impressed, beguiled, frightened, bewildered . . . A considerable achievement"
ANITA BROOKNER

"A fierce, elliptical novel that's both a gripping philosophical thriller and a highly moving meditation on the emotional consequences of war" **MICHIKO KAKUTANI**, *New York Times*

"The narrative is brilliantly complex and beguiling, and the climax devastating" **MIKE PETTY**, *Independent*

"A classic of its kind, brewing up enormous pathos undiluted by sentimentality" **ANTHONY GARDNER**, *Daily Telegraph*

"Clever, highly readable . . . Neither predictable nor surprising, the dénouement, when it finally happens, is shocking, moving and horribly convincing" **MICHAEL ESTORICK**, *Literary Review*

THE LADY IN THE CAR WITH GLASSES AND A GUN

Best crime novel of the year

"Japrisot's story is detailed, substantial, full-blooded. It combines huge intellectual grasp with fascinating narrative, fine writing and an unforgettable protagonist . . . [this] rates as a superb achievement"   EDMUND CRISPIN, *The Times*

"Full of suspense, absorbing, a fast mover . . . this is Japrisot's finest suspense thriller"   *L'Express*

"A cordon bleu mixture of suspense, sex, trick-psychology and fast action"   **Publishers Weekly**

"Another success . . . Sébastien Japrisot has a very personal way of evoking fear"   MARTINE MONOD, *Humanité Dimanche*

To join the mailing list and for a full list of titles please write to

THE HARVILL PRESS
84 THORNHILL ROAD
LONDON N1 1RD, UK

enclosing a stamped-addressed envelope

www.harvill-press.com